"I Want Yo[...]
Whatever [...]

There it was. The [...]
had to accept. Play it cool, she reminded herself. "I already have a job. One I love. With people I respect."

To her surprise Josh Tremont laughed out loud, the sudden sound turning the heads of the diners around them.

"Oh, you're good. It's not everyone who tries to put me in my place so politely. C'mon, name your price."

Callie lifted her gaze to meet his. Instantly she felt the power of his will behind his stare. Were she a weaker woman, she had no doubt she'd have capitulated.

"What if I don't have one?" she finally replied.

"Everybody has a price, Callie," he coaxed.

Dear Reader,

When I wrote the ROGUE DIAMONDS trilogy I had an absolute ball falling in love with each successive hero, but in the last book there was a shadow lurking in the background—a threat to Palmer Enterprises. That threat became so much more than a plot point when I found myself asking, "Who is behind it?" And, more importantly, "Why?"

So I delved a little deeper, and there he was— Josh Tremont, hero in *Defiant Mistress, Ruthless Millionaire*. Josh is one very highly motivated man and he's determined to get the recognition due to him. Writing this book I got to fall in love all over again as I began to fully understand each nuance that made up the complex and driven character Josh became. He wasn't the easiest man to get to know, used as he is to playing his cards from very close to his chest.

Finding the woman who could force his hand, and eventually his heart, open was easy. If you read *Pretend Mistress, Bona Fide Boss,* you'll have met Callie Lee, a steadfast and loyal employee of the Palmer family. Who better to come to their aid and delve into the secrets behind Josh Tremont than her? But Callie discovers more than the truth when she tackles this ruthless millionaire.

I hope you enjoy Josh and Callie's journey to love as they both learn that the truth is not always what you believe it to be.

Happy reading!

Yvonne Lindsay

YVONNE LINDSAY

DEFIANT MISTRESS, RUTHLESS MILLIONAIRE

Silhouette Desire

Published by Silhouette Books

America's Publisher of Contemporary Romance

If you purchased this book without a cover you should be aware
that this book is stolen property. It was reported as "unsold and
destroyed" to the publisher, and neither the author nor the
publisher has received any payment for this "stripped book."

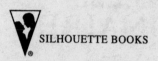 SILHOUETTE BOOKS

ISBN-13: 978-0-373-76986-5

Recycling programs
for this product may
not exist in your area.

DEFIANT MISTRESS, RUTHLESS MILLIONAIRE

Copyright © 2009 by Dolce Vita Trust

All rights reserved. Except for use in any review, the reproduction
or utilization of this work in whole or in part in any form by any
electronic, mechanical or other means, now known or hereafter
invented, including xerography, photocopying and recording, or in
any information storage or retrieval system, is forbidden without
the written permission of the editorial office, Silhouette Books,
233 Broadway, New York, NY 10279 U.S.A.

This is a work of fiction. Names, characters, places and incidents are
either the product of the author's imagination or are used fictitiously, and
any resemblance to actual persons, living or dead, business establishments,
events or locales is entirely coincidental.

This edition published by arrangement with Harlequin Books S.A.

® and TM are trademarks of Harlequin Books S.A., used under license.
Trademarks indicated with ® are registered in the United States Patent
and Trademark Office, the Canadian Trade Marks Office and in other
countries.

Visit Silhouette Books at www.eHarlequin.com

Printed in U.S.A.

Books by Yvonne Lindsay

Silhouette Desire

*The Boss's Christmas Seduction #1758
*The CEO's Contract Bride #1776
*The Tycoon's Hidden Heir #1788
Rossellini's Revenge Affair #1811
Tycoon's Valentine Vendetta #1854
Jealousy & a Jewelled Proposition #1873
Claiming His Runaway Bride #1890
†Convenient Marriage, Inconvenient Husband #1923
†Secret Baby, Public Affair #1930
†Pretend Mistress, Bona Fide Boss #1937
Defiant Mistress, Ruthless Millionaire #1986

*New Zealand Knights
†Rogue Diamonds

YVONNE LINDSAY

New Zealand born to Dutch immigrant parents, Yvonne Lindsay became an avid romance reader at the age of thirteen. Now, married to her "blind date" and with two surprisingly amenable teenagers, she remains a firm believer in the power of romance. Yvonne feels privileged to be able to bring to her readers the stories of her heart. In her spare time, when not writing, she can be found with her nose firmly in a book, reliving the power of love in all walks of life. She can be contacted via her Web site, www.yvonnelindsay.com.

To Diana, for the hand holding and nerve calming
and for dispatching Worry Wilma
back where she belongs, thank you!

One

"I don't feel comfortable with this, Irene."

As soon as the words were out of her mouth Callie knew she'd said the wrong thing. A mere shift in Irene's expression was all it took. A barely perceptible change, but it was enough to forewarn her of her employer's displeasure—displeasure that generally had most staff at Palmer Enterprises scurrying for the nearest hiding place.

"Why is that, Callie?"

"Well," she foundered a moment, lost for words. "Is it even legal? He's bound to want me to sign a confidentiality agreement."

"Should that be your worry?" Irene countered. "As

one of our *valued* employees, you know we'd look after you if there happened to be any fallout."

The older woman's subtle emphasis on the word *valued* sent a chill down Callie's spine. She owed the Palmers—and in particular, Irene Palmer—everything. Without Irene she would have had nothing—not her education, her job, where she lived; even the designer shoes on her feet.

"This works to our advantage, you know," Irene's voice interrupted Callie's thoughts.

"What do you mean?"

Callie looked up at her boss and mentor—the first adult to ever give her hope for a future. The woman who'd actually made her believe she could make something of her life rather than disappear down a drain lined with drugs and crime.

Only no one had ever told her that with debt came a duty to repay it. After twelve years Callie had been forced to ask herself, when would enough be enough?

"Obviously any other time I'd miss having you here as my assistant, but the Guildarian honorary consul position will be announced on Christmas Eve. That's in, what, nine weeks' time?"

Callie nodded, her gaze locked on Irene's face.

"Don't you see, Callie, it's the perfect opportunity. Everyone knows you're my assistant and the whole of New Zealand knows the announcement of Bruce's appointment is only a matter of time. And while it's well documented how fiercely loyal you are to me, when

Bruce and I move to Guildara you will be forced to seek other employment."

At Callie's in-drawn breath, Irene waved a graceful, perfectly manicured hand in the air.

"Yes, I know you expected to head up the new special developments team, but if we don't identify Tremont's mole, and nip his steady undermining of our business firmly in the bud, there won't be a special developments team for you to head because in all likelihood, in a couple of years, there would be no Palmer Enterprises." Irene leaned forward in her chair, her eyes suddenly bright with unexpected tears. "I will do whatever it takes to protect Palmer Enterprises and you're going to help me. This is the ideal opening for you to be seen to be seeking something else."

Callie felt sick to her stomach. She knew Josh Tremont's activities had affected the Palmers—but to the extent that he could destroy the business within a couple of years? Things were worse than she thought.

Inevitability settled like a fatalistic dark cloak around Callie's shoulders.

"So I'm supposed to go in there and spy on him?" She fought to keep her voice level.

"Well, far be it from me to suggest such a thing," Irene blinked back the remnants of weakness in her eyes and composed a smile, the action barely creasing her smooth complexion.

No one would guess, from looking at her, that she was sixty-five. She had the kind of elegant beauty that was timeless, ageless, although there was an air about

her that didn't invite confidences. Not many people
ever got close to Irene. Callie was one of her chosen
few.

"Of course not."

Callie's answering smile was equally lacking in
humour. Irene would never stoop so low as to verbalise such a command, but the implication was clear.

"My dear, you know how grateful we will be," Irene
said with an inclination of her elegantly coiffed head.
"Essentially, you'd still be working for us, just…differ-
ently, that's all. You know I'm not one to over-dramatise
things but, right now, you're our only hope."

Suddenly filled with nervous energy, Callie pushed
up out of her chair and stalked back and forth across
the carpet.

"We don't even know that he's going to offer me a job,"
she blurted. "He only asked me to meet him for lunch."

A small crease formed between Irene's brows.
"Don't be naive, Callie. I taught you better than that.
Of course he's going to offer you a position. It's how
he works. Each one of the key staff he's poached from
us has been invited to lunch with him first. It's not as
if he hides his intentions."

"Does he really believe all he has to do is snap his
fingers and everyone will drop everything to do his
bidding?" Callie responded in impotent frustration.

"Generally, my dear, people do," Irene Palmer observed dryly as she leaned back in her leather executive chair, the serenity on her face giving no clue as to
her thoughts.

"Well, not people like me."

"Which is why this will be all the more convincing. I'm sure I don't need to tell you about how difficult things are in the marketplace right now. Jobs are increasingly hard to come by. And with your position on the verge of disestablishment… Suffice to say that no one would blame you for jumping ship, as it were. Besides, you can't deny that Tremont has a certain magnetism about him."

Callie threw herself back into one of the button-back leather armchairs in front of Irene's desk and sighed. Magnetism. From what she'd heard, Josh Tremont had it in spades. But that didn't mean she wanted to work for him.

"What if, after meeting me, he doesn't want me?"

Irene laughed, the sound like wind rustling through dry leaves in autumn. "Oh, Callie, you underestimate yourself. The man wants you all right."

Something in Irene's voice made Callie stiffen. Just how far did they expect her to go in this spying mission?

More to the point, how far was she prepared to go for the Palmers and for her future?

Two days later, Callie gripped the steering wheel of her late-model hatchback and groaned in frustration. A sleek black Maserati coupe slid neatly into the last parking space in the restaurant car park. Now she'd have to find a parking lot blocks away, and she'd be late.

She hated being late even more than she hated the reason for this meeting.

Her stomach pitched as she recalled what she'd agreed to do. Irene had advised her not to appear too eager initially, in case it might put him off. Well, Callie had no problem with that. She had no respect for the man. None whatsoever. She only hoped that when the offer came she could verbalise the word *yes* when every instinct in her body screamed the opposite.

She reminded herself again of Irene's expectations and why she'd agreed to do this, but it did little to assuage the slow-burning anger that began to seethe deep inside.

She fed the flames by recapping Josh Tremont's insidious methods to undermine the corporate structure at Palmer Enterprises. In the past five years he'd poached several key staff, even going so far as to attempt to buy out their employment contract restraint clauses. When that hadn't worked for the last two executives he'd lured away, he'd simply paid them for the year's standdown period while they languished, ostensibly on holiday, while he'd waited patiently for the months to roll by, secure in the knowledge that Palmers was hurting for their loss.

Now he had his sights set on her.

By the time Callie found a metered car park about three blocks from the restaurant, she'd built up a head of steam to match the rich auburn tint of her hair. She walked with sharp, clipped steps to her destination, oblivious to the catcalls and whistles directed her way from a nearby building site.

She'd deliberately dressed down for the meeting

today, in pencil-slim, chocolate-brown trousers and an apricot, chocolate-and-white-striped, long-sleeved blouse. Never mind that the clothes had cost more than she had ever dreamed she would earn in a week, let alone spend on clothing. To her they screamed blasé, certainly not what one would wear to try to impress a prospective employer of Tremont's calibre. They would set the tone nicely, she thought, with a private smile.

Up until this morning she hadn't been too sure how to play this interview, but on choosing her clothes she'd reached a personal compromise. She didn't want to look too keen, and that certainly wouldn't be difficult, but she didn't want to be too reluctant, either. A balance between the two suited nicely, and if she came off a little brash, well, it wasn't as if he'd withdraw his job offer once he'd made it. He wasn't that kind of man.

Auckland's typically humid spring air had already begun to play havoc with her hair. Wisps that had strategically been pulled free from her ponytail to smoothly frame her face now began to curl flirtatiously. Not exactly the image she'd wanted to project, but short of an interlude in the ladies' room with a hair straightener there was little Callie could do.

Finally, she approached the green canvas awning that heralded the entrance to the restaurant. It was one of Auckland's longest-standing and finest eateries—mind you, she didn't expect anything less from Josh Tremont. A man like him commanded the best at all times, and he wasn't afraid to pay for it. She should feel flattered, she supposed, that he'd requested a meeting with her. Obviously, he thought her integral enough within Palmers that her leaving would cause more of his signature range of trouble.

Callie paused at the threshold to the restaurant lobby. Her reflection in the highly polished glass door showed that, aside from the recalcitrant strands of hair and the slight shine on her nose and cheeks from her power walk to the venue, she looked just fine. She drew in a deep breath and tucked her slim brown Vuitton document case under one arm.

The sudden gloom of the entrance forced Callie to push her sunglasses up onto her head and she scanned the dining room beyond for a sign of Tremont.

"Can I help you, madam?"

Callie fought back a smile at the hoity-toity demeanour of the maitre d'. She doubted he'd be as polite if he knew that twelve years ago she'd dined frequently from the Dumpster at the back of this kitchen and others like it, but then the insides of places like this were all about appearances, and she knew all about how important such appearances were. She arranged her features into a screen of patronising calm before responding.

"I'm meeting Mr Tremont."

"Ah, yes, you must be Ms Lee. Please, come through. Mr Tremont is already waiting."

His implication that she was late and that Mr Tremont wasn't in the habit of being kept waiting was painfully clear in the disdainful glance he cast her. Callie followed the stiff-backed maitre d' as he preceded her through the nearly full dining room, toward a private alcove near the rear. She fought the urge to poke out her tongue at the man's back. But at the sage old age of twenty-eight she knew better than to give in to impulses that could lead you into trouble.

"Ms Lee for you, sir."

Callie had seen pictures of Josh Tremont in the gossip columns as well as in business magazines, but she was unprepared for the sizzling power of being pinned by his electric-blue eyes when he lifted his gaze from the PDA in his hand. Now she knew what people meant when they referred to that "caught in the head-lights" moment. That time in space when you froze, unsure of whether to flee or fight.

She'd come prepared for the latter, but face-to-face with the man himself she wished she'd been in a position to have refused his invitation outright. A flutter of something she didn't want to admit might be attrac-tion shifted in the pit of her belly.

"Mr Tremont," Callie said, deciding to take the initiative and offer her hand.

Josh Tremont uncrossed his leg and placed his PDA on the crisp white linen tablecloth in front of him before standing to accept her hand. Callie's heart jumped a beat as his long fingers closed around hers and irration-ally she wondered how his hands would feel on other parts of her body. Strong, capable, warm. Another tiny pull threaded through her body and yanked, hard.

No wonder the man featured so widely in all the papers. His allure was overwhelming and, she realised, he'd yet to utter a single word.

He let go of her hand and gestured to the seat opposite, waiting for the maitre d' to pull out her chair and see her settled before he sat again himself.

The dark silver-grey suit he wore, teamed with a black shirt and tie, befitted his outlaw-type dark good looks. And, even though it was only one in the afternoon, already he'd begun to sport a shadow on his cheeks—just enough to take the completely polished edge off the man who she knew was ranked right up there on New Zealand's rich list.

"I'm pleased you could make it, Callie Rose."

Callie stiffened in her chair as his deep voice washed over her like a brush of warm velvet.

"Only those close to me call me Callie Rose," she said firmly, determined to draw her line in the sand as quickly as possible. "You may call me Callie, or Ms Lee."

The slow smile that spread across his face was mesmerising. Genuine humour sparked in his eyes, tiny lines appearing at the corners, before the corners of his sensually shaped lips pulled into a curve. He bent his head slightly in acknowledgement.

"Callie," he smiled fully now, the full strength of his charisma aimed front and centre. "Can I offer you something to drink before lunch?"

"Just iced mineral water, thank you."

She kept her posture upright, her features schooled into an expression of polite disinterest. She would not smile back at him. She. Would. Not.

The man was unscrupulous. Unscrupulous and highly

intelligent, and with every business coup he success-fully completed he threatened Palmer Enterprises just that much more. She would have to work hard to make him believe he would be using her as his latest stepping-stone to usurping Palmers' position rather than the other way around.

He placed their order for drinks—to her surprise, ordering the same beverage for himself.

"You don't need to drink water just because I am," she said.

"Oh, don't worry. I don't do anything just to make someone else comfortable," he answered, pinning her with that gaze once more. "Unless absolutely necessary, of course."

The way his voice dropped an octave on the last few words sent a shiver across her skin and Callie had no trouble imagining what situation "absolutely neces-sary" encompassed. A visual image of bare skin against bare skin, of the warm touch of a gentle palm, of legs entwined, burned across her eyes.

Heat gathered deep inside her, slowly unfurling through her lower extremities and making her want to shift in her seat. Instead, she reached for the mineral water that had thankfully been promptly delivered, and took a long cooling sip.

"Thirsty?"

There was an edge of humour to Tremont's voice that slid under her skin to irritate.

"Yes, actually," she answered. "I had quite a walk to get here, and it's warm outside."

"Oh? No parks left?"

"No. Someone in an overpriced set of wheels took the last space." A cold finger of caution traced a line down Callie's spine but she already knew it was too late, darn it. Inwardly, she sighed. "It was you, wasn't it?"

"Guilty as charged." He put both hands up in a gesture of surrender. "But if I'd have known I was putting you out I would have left it for you."

"No problem. I'm not afraid of a bit of exercise."

She hadn't meant her words to be an invitation to him to check her out, but he did. His gaze gliding over her shoulders, her breasts and lower to where her long legs were crossed to one side of the table.

"No," he said softly. "I'm sure you're not. But still, it would be a shame to damage those pretty sandals you're wearing. Manolos, right? I'll drop you back to your car after lunch. Think of it as atonement."

"Really, that won't be necessary."

She was taken aback that he'd recognised the brand of her shoes. Shoes were her greatest weakness, and considering the years she'd gone either barefoot, or clad in ill-fitting shoes purloined from clothing recycle bins, it was a miracle her feet were even in any kind of condition to be showcased in such extravagant splendour.

"We'll see," he answered enigmatically. "Now, I'm sure your time is precious. Why don't you choose what you'd like for lunch and we'll get down to business."

When she was ready, he summoned their waiter over. Callie requested a Caesar salad and he ordered steamed salmon with glazed asparagus tips.

"Tell me, Callie, how long have you worked for the Palmers?"

Tremont sat back in his seat, one arm slung across the wide back of the chair in a move clearly designed to be casual and to invite confidence. The look on his face, however, was anything but. Callie recognised the keen perusal he gave her as he assessed her body language and prepared to process her response. She finally allowed herself to smile as she leaned forward and rested her elbows on the table, clasping her hands lightly together. Let him make from that what he wanted, she thought.

"Since I finished my communications degree," she answered, deliberately not being specific about when that had occurred.

Tremont nodded before speaking again.

"I understand you completed your master's with honours—that's no small feat."

She fought to conceal her surprise. Given his response he knew full well when she'd attended university. He was just playing her. It was really no more than she'd expected, she reminded herself, and she was prepared.

"That's right," she said carefully. "But since you already know all that, why don't you ask me something you don't know?"

A flare of blue flame lit in his eyes and he lifted a hand to stroke the edge of his jaw.

"What would it take to win you over, Callie?"

"Win me over? I think you need to be more specific."

"Now, I know you're an intelligent woman, and I also know that you're fully aware of the general exodus of staff from Palmer Enterprises to Tremont Corporation."

Callie nodded, barely trusting herself to speak for fear that she'd let her anger bubble over.

"I wouldn't call it a general exodus, exactly," she managed through tight lips. "Some of us are still loyal."

"Ah," he smiled. "Implying that you are unswerving in your devotion?"

"You think there's a problem with that?" She leaned back in her chair and crossed her arms, uncaring as to what he analysed by her body language now. "Seems you ought to be more concerned about the loyalty of people you can buy."

Twin creases formed between Tremont's heavy black brows and his eyes grew distant. This was the real Josh Tremont, she reminded herself. This was the man who cold-bloodedly bought information about Palmer Enterprises and used it to his advantage to underbid or outsupply their clients—bit by bit, year by year, eating away at their success.

"Good point," he conceded. Before he could say any more, the waiter brought their plates. "Let's leave this discussion until we've eaten, hmm? Wouldn't want to spoil your appetite."

Callie allowed herself a short laugh. "It'd take a lot more than conversation to spoil my appetite."

"I'm pleased to hear it," he smiled in return. "I enjoy a woman with healthy appetites."

Callie froze; her fork halfway to her mouth. She had no doubt what appetites he was talking about. Again that image flashed before her eyes, this time though it was *her* body, *her* skin that he touched. And, as if he'd reached across the table and stroked his elegant hand across her shoulder and down, she felt her breasts grow full and heavy—her nipples beading into tight points, abrading the soft fabric of her bra.

She was relieved when he skilfully turned the conversation to more general matters while they ate, and she was surprised to find herself enjoying his sharp wit and broad opinions as they ranged across a variety of topics.

It was only after the waiter had cleared away their plates and delivered frothy cappuccinos that Callie began to relax. She picked up her teaspoon and scooped the chocolate off the froth of her coffee. She lifted it to her lips and her tongue darted out to savour the hint of wickedness—her favourite indulgence during the week. Tremont's next words, however, brought things firmly back to business.

"I want you, Callie, and I'll pay whatever it takes to get you."

There it was. The offer she dreaded but knew she had to accept. She remembered her discussion with Irene earlier in the week. Play it cool, she reminded herself.

Callie raised one eyebrow in response. "I already have a job. One I love. With people I respect."

To her surprise Josh Tremont laughed out loud, the sudden sound turning the heads of the diners around them.

"Oh, you're good, Callie. You're very good. It's not everyone who tries to put me in my place so politely. C'mon, name your price."

Callie took a sip of her coffee then carefully replaced her cup on its saucer and lifted her gaze to meet his. Instantly she felt the power of his will behind his stare. Were she a weaker woman, or even someone who owed the Palmers any less, she had no doubt she'd have capitulated. But she wasn't that person and she owed them everything. Nothing he could do, or offer, would change that.

"What if I don't have one?" she finally replied.

"Everybody has a price, Callie," he coaxed.

"Let me think about it. I'll call you," she smiled coolly as she rose and collected her document case. "Thank you very much for lunch. I believe our meeting is over."

She tucked her case back under one arm before extending her hand to Tremont to say goodbye. He got up from his chair, a dangerous glitter reflected in his eyes. He took her hand, his thumb rubbing gently across her skin, sending a ripple of warmth to traverse up her arm.

"I haven't given up, you know. Didn't your mother ever warn you about men like me? We enjoy a challenge."

Callie thought briefly of the woman who'd given birth to her. A woman who'd preferred to dish out abuse—physical or mental, she hadn't been fussy—rather than advice of any kind.

He leaned in a little closer. "I'll let you go for now, but don't keep me waiting too long," he urged, releasing her hand.

YVONNE LINDSAY   23

"I said I'll think about it. I won't promise more than that."

Tremont gave a short sharp nod. "I'll take you back to your car."

"That won't be necessary."

"I said I'd take you back to your car, and I will. I'm a man of my word."

"Are you?" she jibed.

"Oh, yes. Don't mistake me, Callie. I say what I mean and I always get what I want. Eventually."

Two

Josh Tremont set his phone back down on his desk and leaned back in his chair, swivelling it around to view the glittering panorama of Auckland City's inner harbour. For a moment he savoured the taste of success before his mind turned to analysing the call he'd just received.

He allowed a small smile to pull at his lips. So Callie Rose Lee had her price after all. It was high, but he could afford it. Besides, she was worth so much more to him than she could possibly realise. She'd been groomed by the Palmer family for the past ten years and losing her would hopefully send a shock wave through them that would reverberate for some time. And into the bargain he got an exceptionally clever, and beautiful, assistant.

Now the last pieces of his plan would fall into place just the way he wanted. This way, at least, he could get right down to business instead of wasting precious time wooing her away from Irene Palmer's clawlike grip. The satisfaction that spread through him was a balm to his soul.

Josh got up from his seat and crossed to the shelving unit against his office wall. He lifted a photo frame from the wooden shelf and stared at the faded black-and-white picture within. His mother looked so happy in this shot—so carefree—and, with her hand on his eight-year-old shoulder, they'd faced the world believing everything was good in their lives. But it had been a lie. Nothing about his upbringing had been what it seemed, nor what it should have been—now all that was about to change.

Bruce Palmer had had his opportunity to make a difference and he'd chosen not to. Had chosen instead the unemotional frozen woman who ruled his empire at his side. Had chosen his legal-born son over his illegitimate bastard.

Palmer's curt dismissal of Josh's notification when his mother had died—a single sheet of paper with "No contact" typed in bold black letters—had sealed his fate. Then eighteen, Josh had been shocked to finally discover who his father really was and the searing pain of emphatic rejection, hard on the heels of the death of the only parent he had ever known, had been the catalyst that continued to drive him.

If Palmer had been half the man the country believed he was Josh's mother wouldn't have had to work up to three jobs at a time to make sure Josh never missed out.

In return, he'd vowed that one day he'd make things right for her and give her the luxuries she deserved. Sadly, her illness had denied him the chance to ever spoil her. Josh still cursed himself that, wrapped up in his studies, he hadn't noticed her slow deterioration or realised that her perpetual weariness was a far more ominous indicator than simply her body's response to the physical demands of her work.

The doctors had said it was too late to do anything for her by the time they'd detected the cancer. Too late to do anything but hope against hope that she wouldn't slip away while he was at school during the day, or at the cleaning job he'd taken over from her late at night to help cover their living costs.

She'd lingered for two years and her end, when it came, had been without him by her side. He'd been at the graduation ceremony for school, where he'd been awarded top honours in his year group and a scholarship to attend Victoria University in Wellington, only a short journey from their home.

He'd felt the emptiness the instant he'd set foot inside the door, both in the house and in his heart. An emptiness that remained, locked deep inside.

His fingers tightened around the frame, knuckles whitening as the helpless rage that had filled him as an angry and confused teen came rushing back. He forced himself to relax and carefully replaced the photo on the shelf, then closed his eyes for a moment, allowing the happier image to imprint over the one that always lingered in the back of his mind.

The instant he had his fury under control again his eyes snapped open and his gaze drifted to the Palmer Enterprises building, only a couple of blocks away, framed by his window. Yes, Bruce Palmer would pay for his callous choice, and he'd pay dearly. By the time Josh was finished with him the older man would know the pain of regret and Josh's thirst for payback would finally be quenched.

Josh moved back to his desk and opened the computer file he had on Callie, his eyes roaming the head-and-shoulders shot of her that filled his screen.

His insides clenched as he observed the tilt of her head, the tint of red in her long hair hinting at the fiery potential in her temper. The picture, however, hadn't captured the essence of her as a woman. She'd controlled herself so well at lunch the other week, but the hint of anger in her chocolate-brown eyes had barely veiled what he believed was the true level of passion in her nature. Callie Rose Lee in the flesh was an entirely more enticing package than the computer screen promised.

"So that's the tour of the office complex all done!"

The fresh-faced staffer who'd shown Callie around Tremont's high rise turned with a smile that almost made Callie feel like she was waiting for applause or a pat on the head for a job well done.

"Thank you, Sabrina. It certainly was comprehensive."

So comprehensive, in fact, Callie wondered when she'd ever actually get to start some work. The tour had taken the entire morning and she'd yet to meet up with Josh Tremont again or see where she'd be working herself.

"Ah, here's Mr Tremont now. Right on time."

Callie stiffened, every nerve in her body going onto full alert. By the look on Sabrina's face, she had a serious case of hero worship. Callie stifled a groan and cursorily reminded herself why she was really here.

"Callie, good to see you. I had a meeting this morning but I'm sure Sabrina has taken good care of you."

Josh Tremont extended his hand and after the briefest hesitation Callie took it. Instantly his fingers curled warmly around her hand, enveloping her with his strength. She was glad he wasn't one of those men who insisted on either squeezing the bejeezus out of your fingers or dominating the handshake with his hand on top.

No, men like Josh Tremont didn't need those tactics to show who was in charge. It was clear in the look he gave her as he welcomed her into his domain—powerful, omnipotent. A chill rippled a shiver of warning down her spine and she forced back a shudder. She was truly in the lion's den now.

He was dressed today in a black blazer teamed with sharply pressed grey trousers and a crisp white shirt. His blue tie, hand-dyed silk if her eye wasn't mistaken, sat in a perfect Windsor knot, and reflected the colour of his eyes. He could have stepped straight off the pages of *GQ* magazine.

Callie slowly became aware that he still held her hand. The warmth of his grasp permeated her skin and sent a tiny flare of something hotter spiraling deep inside her. She pulled away with as much decorum as she could muster but not soon enough to stop the tingle that registered just beneath her palm. She stroked her hand down over her hip, over the hem of her sensible cream-coloured business jacket and the slim fit of her matching trousers, but it did nothing to assuage the sensation that his hand still clasped hers.

"Are you ready to see where you'll be working while we're based in the office?"

"I certainly am," Callie answered, determined to at least appear to be keen on her new role even if her insides were clattering away like a flock of nervous parrots.

"Follow me," Josh gestured toward an elevator bank and pulled a swipe key from his belt as they entered the waiting lift.

"Thanks again for showing me around," Callie said to Sabrina.

The other girl gave her a smile and a wave and started to walk away as the lift doors closed. As lifts went, the car was bigger than many she'd been in, but for some reason the walls seemed closer than they should be. Josh Tremont seemed closer. Was it her imagination or had he moved in to be nearer to her as the car travelled up to what was tagged as the executive floor?

His cologne tantalised her, a hint of black pepper and

sandalwood mixed with something else. Whatever it was, it played havoc with her equilibrium. Thankfully, the journey upward was swift and, as the lift doors slid silently open, Callie let go the breath she'd unconsciously held.

"Our senior executives are all housed on this floor, together with our legal department. You'll be issued your own security clearance and swipe key. Every key access is logged and counterchecked by security on a regular basis to provide a complete record of our staff movements."

"That way no one is where they shouldn't be?" Callie asked. Maybe this was going to be a whole lot tougher than she anticipated.

"As I'm sure you're aware from your previous work, in these competitive times security and confidentiality are paramount."

Oh, yes, she knew it all right. And while Josh Tremont was clearly a stickler for guarding his own turf, he wasn't above stealing or buying information about others.

"I'm surprised you don't have everyone fitted with a personal tracking device," she said with a light laugh.

"Don't be. I've thought about it. But this does just as well."

Josh pressed his index finger on a reader set in a panel on the wall beside enormous double doors. A green light flashed on the display of the reader and the doors swung open, revealing a massive office suite.

"You use biometric identification on this floor?"

"And in our IT section, yes. By the end of next year, we'll use it through the whole building."

Callie followed Josh inside, and tried to quell the sense of disquiet that threaded through her as the doors swung closed behind them—much like the solid gates of an olde worlde stronghold. It didn't take too much imagination to connect the dots and cast her new employer in the role of lord of this particular manor.

Josh gestured toward a modern workstation. "This is where you'll be working." He pulled out the chair, inviting her to sit down. "You'll see there's another print reader associated with your computer. Drew, my head of IT, will be up shortly to log you in to the system."

Callie sat upright in the chair, not daring to let her back brush against the top where she sensed Josh's hand had settled. She nodded toward the closed office doors. "Are they always kept shut?"

"Absolutely. When someone comes, they'll appear on your screen via the intranet CCTV system. If they're already recorded in our database, a brief bio will pop up next to their picture. If they don't have an appointment, they don't come in. Mind you, they'd be hard pressed to get this far without security clearance anyway."

The opening credits of old *Get Smart* episodes flitted through her mind.

"Is all the security really necessary?"

Josh barked a short laugh and leaned forward a little. "You worked at Palmer Enterprises. You tell me."

Callie fought back the retort that sprang to her lips. She had to remind herself yet again that for all intents and purposes she was now working for Tremont Corporation. More specifically, for the man himself.

She looked up toward him and forced a smile. "I see your point."

"I thought you might."

Her breath suddenly stilled in her chest as he smiled at her in return. A genuine smile—one that lit his eyes and caused laugh lines to fan out at their corners. She felt her own lips curve more generously in response and saw his gaze drop to her mouth, saw the light in his eyes spark into something more, something that made her suddenly wish she wasn't here under false pretences.

Callie turned her head. She couldn't afford to let him see the truth in her eyes. She'd promised Irene she would do everything in her power to unearth the mole at Palmer Enterprises and she darn well would get the job done, no matter how charismatic Josh Tremont proved to be. She forced her attention back to the job.

"So I can't log in to the system until Drew has been here?"

Josh hesitated before answering and she felt him shift away—ever so slightly, but it was enough to create the illusion of a little more breathing space between them.

"Correct, and as much as I admire your eagerness to get to work I thought you might like to have some lunch with me first." He straightened and stepped toward another set of tall double doors. "Come. I had the restaurant send up a light buffet for us."

"What about Drew?"

"I'll get the alert in my office when he arrives."

Callie rose and followed Josh through to his office. She gasped as they entered. The floor-to-ceiling windows offered a near seamless view of the central business district and then up the inner city harbour. She almost felt as if she could step off the carpet and straight into the air over the glistening waters. But there, smack in the centre of the CBD, stood the Palmer building. It was as if he could peer down through the tinted glass and see right inside from here.

A frisson of disquiet pricked at her senses. One that made her wonder if it was more than just business rivalry that had Tremont Corporation a step ahead of the Palmers at almost every turn. But that was ridiculous. Virtually everything about the Palmers' world was public knowledge and there were no skeletons in their closets.

"Stunning, isn't it? I never tire of the view. You almost feel as if you own it all."

He'd moved in close behind her. So close she could feel his breath on the back of her neck. Rather than intimidate, it sent little sparks of flame licking along her skin. This was crazy, Callie thought, he isn't even touching me and I… She jammed a lid on the notion before it could form fully in her mind, because if it did, she'd be admitting to an attraction she knew she should never act on nor reveal.

She wasn't here to have a mutually satisfying fling—although Josh Tremont was very much the kind of man that spoke to her femininity. He was strong, and without a shadow of a doubt he was good looking, but above all that he had an aura of survival that appealed to her on a level that went beyond the instinctive. For that reason, if not her promise to Irene, she knew she couldn't succumb to his charm.

She'd trained herself to make her choices based on rational thought, not on gut feeling. She would not change that now, not for anything or anyone.

Callie stepped sideways to put some space between them, and turned away from the window. She allowed herself a steadying breath before she could trust herself to speak.

"Yes, the view is quite spectacular. How on earth do you get any work done?"

"It's my motivation to work."

"How so?"

"I've seen worse things and I have no desire to see them again."

Callie nodded. "I know what you mean."

She risked a look at Josh, surprised to find him already staring at her, a considering look in his eyes. His wide, sensually shaped lips curved into a smile.

"Yes. Yes, you would."

His voice reverberated in the space between them, stroking her barely controlled senses back into full flame. A flame that died out just as rapidly. He knew *that* much about her?

"Funny thing, don't you think?" he continued. "The harder we work for what we have, the more determined we become to hold on to it."

She stiffened. He struck a little too close to her core. She summoned a noncommittal response and it must have sufficed because he gestured to the sideboard across the office where silver chafing dishes emitted a delicious aroma. Crockery and cutlery were stacked to one side.

Josh walked over and grabbed one of the white bone china plates and handed it to her.

"Here, would you like me to serve?"

Callie's fingers brushed his as she took the proffered plate.

"No, thanks. I'll serve myself."

"Are you always this independent?" Josh asked, cocking his head slightly to one side as if he were still assessing her and hadn't quite found the right-shaped hole for her particular peg.

Callie allowed herself a smile. "Yes, always."

Josh gave her a small nod. "Duly noted."

They were eating their lunch, a light Thai green curry with fluffy jasmine rice and salad, when an alert sounded on Josh's computer.

"That's Drew."

He buzzed the other man in and walked through to the main office to greet him. Callie placed her plate down on the coffee table in front of her and stood as they came into Josh's office.

"Callie, I'd like you to meet Drew Grant. He's head of IT here at Tremont Corp and what he doesn't know on the subject isn't worth knowing."

High praise indeed from a man who had a reputation for demanding excellence. Callie reached out to shake Drew's hand.

"Pleased to meet you." She smiled.

"Welcome to Tremont Corp," he replied with a smile that transformed his long, thin face from intensity to a warm friendliness.

"Drew, have some lunch with us, then you can get Callie into the system and run her through the basics of our programmes."

Josh settled onto the couch right next to where Callie was sitting. If Callie hadn't known better, she would have thought he was staking his claim against any potential interest from the other man. His knee brushed against the fabric of her pants and she surreptitiously inched away from the contact.

She was no man's possession, no matter how powerful he thought he was or how much he'd agreed to pay her.

Once Drew had filled a plate and joined them, Josh asked him to explain the basics behind the systems the company used. Callie listened carefully, all the time hyperconscious of the man at her side. Josh said very little as Drew covered the practicalities of what she would be able to do on her computer. Despite their system being vastly different from that at Palmers, she knew she'd master it in no time and, in fact, she was eager to get started. An eagerness that was beginning to have more to do with her reaction to her proximity to her new boss, than a desire to work.

"We may as well get into it, then," she said with what

she hoped was sufficient professional eagerness, and she rose to take her plate over to the sideboard.

Instantly she felt the loss of his presence beside her. She pushed the sensation aside. He was a man, albeit a powerful one, but still just a man and she'd vowed long ago never to fall victim again to one man's power over her.

"Good idea," Josh agreed. "You all ready to go, Drew?"

"Ready as ever. Thanks for the lunch."

As Callie and Drew left the inner sanctum of Josh's office, she felt his eyes bore a hole in the back of her head. She clenched her hands into tight fists at her sides, determined not to reach up and scratch the itch left there. It was a relief to be out of his sight and settled at her desk.

By the time Drew left her, with a reassurance that he was only a phone call away, she felt more than able to tackle whatever Josh sent her way. How she would tackle her reaction to him was another matter entirely.

Three

From the door to his inner office Josh watched Callie at work. She was totally absorbed in her task, her eyes never straying from the flat-screen monitor, her fingers flying over her keyboard as if they had minds of their own.

She wore her hair up in a tight twist, exposing the long slender curve of her neck, the gentle sweep of her jaw. Something hot and tight clenched low in his gut. Having her here was playing with fire—he'd sworn that he'd never indulge in an office romance the way his mother and father had—but Josh hadn't got where he was today by playing it safe.

Her first week at Tremont Corporation had flown by,

and now that they were at the end of week two his attraction to her had only grown more intense. He wasn't going to ignore it any longer and rationalised that the hit to Palmers would be twofold when he and Callie became a couple, and he had no doubt they would. Not only had they lost a pivotal staff member but seeing her on his arm in the society pages would just be rubbing salt into the wound.

Josh cleared his throat and allowed a small smile of satisfaction to curl his lips as she startled and stopped what she was doing.

"Callie, I need you to attend a gallery opening and silent auction with me tonight. I hope you're free."

Too bad if she wasn't, she'd simply have to change her plans. Under his perusal he saw her eyes widen in surprise for the briefest moment before she appeared to gather her thoughts.

"Tonight?"

"Tremont Corp has sponsored a new gallery in conjunction with the Blackthorne School of Fine Arts."

"That's the school that offers scholarships to kids from underprivileged backgrounds, isn't it?"

Kids like he'd been. "Yeah, that's the one. I'll pick you up around seven. Dress formal."

Callie visibly bristled at his preemptory tone. "I haven't said I'm free yet."

He was beginning to enjoy seeing how he could unsettle her. Each day brought its own new challenge with Callie. He kept his face poker straight as he answered.

"If you're not, you'll have to change your plans. I need you there."

Need being a relative word. He *wanted* her there with him.

"Why wasn't this in the appointment schedule?"

Good question, he conceded silently. "I hadn't made up my mind to attend until just now. Do you have any objection?"

"I object to the lack of notice, but as it happens I am free this evening."

Josh nodded. "Get used to things happening without notice. One of the duties I demand from my staff is flexibility and availability. I'll be at your place at seven— I already know where you live. Be ready."

Josh drew his Maserati to a halt outside the compact two-story town house Callie had listed as her residence. The brick-and-weatherboard building was well maintained, and the garden lining the front path was full of late spring colour with the kind of plants his mother had always adored. It was a far cry from the manicured perfection showcasing the palatial 1920s mansion he called home in St Heliers.

Still, considering her location here in Mt Eden, she was doing pretty well for herself. He wondered how much of her position she'd achieved on her own and how much had been assisted by the Palmer family. They tended to look after their own—when it suited them.

With long practice he quelled the habitual anger that flooded his mind. Things should have been so different for his mother and for him as he grew up. The reminder of what the Palmers were capable of never lay far from the periphery of his mind, even if they'd successfully hoodwinked the nation into believing they were squeaky-clean paragons of society.

Payback would be an absolute bitch. He would personally make certain of that.

His hand hovered at the wood-panelled front door to knock, but before his knuckles could rap against the varnished surface the door swung open.

Not a lot took Josh's breath away these days, but the vision of elegant sophistication in front of him managed to succeed where many had failed.

At first he thought her halter-neck gown was black, but in the overhead lighting he realised it was a rich dark chocolate brown—the same colour as her eyes. The fabric skimmed over her body, in much the same way his fingers now itched to do, caressing each curve in a subtle yet sensuous sweep.

He let out a long low-pitched whistle.

"You look amazing."

"Thank you. You did say formal. I hope this isn't too much."

Too much? He stepped back to appreciate the rear view of the dress as she came through the doorway and methodically locked her front door. The creamy skin of her back was exposed until just below her shoulder blades, and for some reason he found what the gown hid even more enticing than what it revealed.

"It's perfect. Thank you."

"For getting it right?" Callie looked up at him from sexy smoky-shadowed eyes.

"Yes."

"Believe me, I've been well trained."

There was a note to her voice he couldn't put his finger on. Not quite strain, not quite cynicism, either.

Josh felt his lips curve into a smile. "I can well imagine."

Callie stiffened at his side. "What do you mean by that?"

"The Palmers expect a certain, shall we say, level of behaviour in their consorts."

"As do you," she was quick to retort.

"As do I," he conceded with a small nod of his head. He placed his hand on the small of her back. "Come, let's get going."

She didn't move immediately and he wondered if she thought he was being too informal touching her as he did, but her lips firmed slightly, as if she'd come to some silent decision, and she allowed him to guide her back down her pathway toward his waiting car.

Beneath his hand the silky fabric of her gown shifted with each step she took, the movement barely detectable but enough to set up a hum of electricity tingling across his palm. It would be no hardship to ease the sensation by stroking his hand across the gentle curve of her hip, but he knew he wouldn't give in to the elemental urge. Not this time.

At his car he swung open the passenger door and waited as she settled into the leather seat and scooped the skirt of her dress inside so it was clear of the door-frame.

Her slender feet were wrapped in a web of delicate bronze leather straps, her toenails painted vermilion. The tingle of electricity that had started on his hand gathered momentum and sent a jolt of something stronger straight to his groin. Man, she had sexy feet. He'd never thought of himself as a foot kind of guy, but when it came to the parade of footwear Callie wore he'd been easily swung over.

"Nice shoes," he commented after he'd shut her door and settled into the driver's seat beside her.

"Thank you." A wry smile played around her glossy lips, lips he imagined would feel as soft and tender as they looked. "Shoes are a bit of a weakness of mine," she admitted.

"I noticed," Josh laughed, determined to put her at ease tonight.

"Ah, well, I suppose we all have our vices. What's yours?"

Her question hung in the air between them. What would she do, he wondered, if he admitted his? Instead, he replied smoothly, "I have no vices."

Her snort of disbelief was barely audible.

"What?" he asked. "You think I do?"

"I don't know you well enough to comment."

"But you've heard rumours," he pressed.

"Some, however I'm not in the habit of forming opinions based on rumour."

"An admirable quality," Josh conceded.

"One of my many," she replied in that tone she'd used at the front door.

He put that thought away to examine later. Callie Lee was proving to have intriguingly hidden depths he hadn't anticipated. Much as he hadn't anticipated the alluring draw of her sensuality. The fact that she was oblivious to it made her even more tempting, and she was a temptation he would succumb to—all in good time.

Callie watched as people swirled about the gallery. Most were more interested in being noticed among the Who's Who of Auckland's glitterati than in the quality of the art on display. She'd done the rounds as Josh's assistant, ensuring that the right sponsors rubbed shoulders with the right beneficiaries, that those who were only there for a free ride got what they wanted before being carefully shunted away from the main rooms.

She'd finally taken a few minutes to peruse the works around the room herself, prior to the speeches she knew Josh would lead before the auction results were announced. She paused in front of a small oil painting. The subject in the picture was faceless but dejection was evident in the slant of the subject's shoulders. It could have been a boy or a girl—it didn't matter.

Callie felt a wrench deep in her heart at the picture. She remembered that feeling. The desolation. The despair. An invisible fist closed around her throat and the burn of tears welled up in the back of her eyes. The artist had done more than view the subject. Given the kids this evening was designed to support, she had no doubt the artist *was* the subject.

"Powerful, isn't it?"

Josh's deep voice, close to her ear, made her start in surprise. Last she'd seen he'd been three deep in discussions with some of the biggest names in New Zealand industry. The Palmers were, of course, notably absent.

She nodded, her throat still too choked to speak, but his next words startled her even more.

"Are you going to bid on it?"

She turned to face him. "Are you kidding? I can't compete with the people here." She smiled deprecatingly. "I'm not in their league."

Josh appeared to consider her for a while before he tilted his head to one side. "No, you're not, are you?"

Even though she'd set herself up for his response she couldn't help but bristle. Words formed on the tip of her tongue, but before she could give them voice he continued.

"You have many more layers to you, don't you, Callie? You should bid on the painting. You might be surprised to see what happens," he finished enigmatically before acknowledging the hail of a well-dressed couple across the gallery floor. "Excuse me."

He was gone as quickly as he'd appeared at her side and Callie turned back to the picture, her teeth catching at her lower lip as she studied it again. That she wanted it was undeniable. The child on the canvas could have been her. She let her gaze roam over the colours and textures of the picture, away from the central focus and to the outer range.

And there she noticed a golden glow, a faint ray of sunshine slanting across the sky; on the bare tree branches were the tiniest of green buds. Of growth and renewal. Of hope.

For the first time in many years Callie suddenly felt completely inadequate. She'd have given her entire collection of shoes to be able to bid what this painting was worth to her on a personal level. Even then she'd barely scrape the surface. No, no matter how much she wanted it, there was no way she could reasonably bid on the picture. Anything less than five figures would be laughable in an atmosphere like tonight's.

With the discipline of years of practice, Callie resolutely turned her back on the picture and on all it portrayed.

The balance of the evening continued smoothly, but her feet had begun to ache in their designer splendour by the time the silent auction winners were to be announced. Many guests had moved on to other, more social, activities, and the gallery no longer seethed with the press of those who wanted to be seen to be doing the right thing. Callie let a sigh of relief slide from her lungs. The evening would be over soon enough and she'd be home.

Josh was up on the podium, ready to complete his part in the formalities, and his commanding presence brought the room to a hush. From her vantage point near the back, Callie let her gaze roam over him. He was all too easy on the eye. He spoke for fifteen minutes, although it felt more like five as his deep, strong voice held the attention of the guests effortlessly and she found herself falling under his spell. He outlined the purpose of the gallery and pledged Tremont Corporation's renewed financial support to the scholarship fund—all to great applause.

After handing the proceedings over to the gallery director, he threaded through the crowd to where she stood.

"Come on, let's go," he said, bending his head to speak quietly in her ear.

"But the auction results," Callie protested.

"Does it matter? Did you bid on *Hope?*"

"*Hope?*"

"The oil you were studying earlier."

"No."

Josh gave her one of his rare smiles, the type that appeared to shine from deep in his blue eyes, as if he could see directly into her soul. "Why not?"

Callie paused under the intensity of Josh's gaze, unsure of what to say or what to do. Her pulse kicked up a beat and her lips and throat suddenly felt dry. The noise of the crowd around them faded away until the only person in the room with her was Josh. The entrancing scent of his cologne drifted around her, luring her into its sensual snare. Eventually, she managed to force her words past her lips.

"To be honest, I didn't think I could bid high enough to do the artist justice."

Josh stepped in closer, his arm sliding around her waist, his hand resting on her hip—burning a brand of possession she didn't want to argue.

"I know what you mean. Let's head out, then, hmm?"

He guided her out of the gallery. Once past the crowds, his arm dropped back away from her side, and suddenly she felt as if she'd been cast adrift. It had been all too easy to fall into step with him, to savour the brush of his hip and thigh against her own, as they walked from the gallery. But she'd been imagining there had been more between them. She was there to do a job—specifically, a job for his uncontested rival. A tremor of regret rippled through her.

"Cold?" Josh asked as one of the parking valets brought his car purring around to the front of the building.

"No, I'm fine."

But she was anything but fine. Tonight had proven that no matter how hard she'd fought against it in the office, she was painfully and irrevocably drawn to her boss—and that made what she was there to do, and the time in which she had left to do it, doubly more difficult.

She was silent on the journey home. Oblivious to the streaking lights passing them by from other vehicles along the road. It wasn't long before they pulled up outside her town house. Josh turned off the ignition, the growl of the Maserati's motor lingering like a discordant echo in the still night air.

YVONNE LINDSAY   49

"Thank you for this evening," Callie said, opening the door herself and alighting from the car as quickly as she could.

She didn't want to wait for him to step around the vehicle and open her door or even have him touch her, because she didn't want to question too deeply what she'd do if she did.

She'd been working for him for a fortnight now. Two weeks where she'd done her best to complete her tasks to the highest standards. Fourteen days where—instead of looking for an avenue to lead to answers as to who the Palmer Enterprises leak was—she'd been battling her growing attraction to a man who was, without a doubt, the one person on this planet to whom she shouldn't be drawn.

Callie started up the path to her front door. She heard Josh's car door open, then another sound. Her key was in her hand. Only another couple of metres more and she'd be inside.

"Callie, hold up a minute. I have something for you."

Josh's voice arrested her retreat and she took a breath to quell the sudden butterflies that rose in a maddening flock from the pit of her stomach. She turned to face him.

Her eyes widened as she saw the "something" he'd mentioned. A flat rectangle, wrapped in brown paper.

"I know I didn't give you a whole lot of notice about tonight. I'd like you to have this, as a token of my appreciation."

"That's not necessary. You pay me well for my job. I—"

"Callie," he interrupted. "Take the damn parcel, okay?"

Callie's eyes locked with his and beneath the blue depths she saw something more than what had been there earlier. Gone was the lazy humour. Instead, it was replaced by a blazing blue flame. His eyes dropped to her mouth and the flame burned brighter, before meeting her gaze again. As if under his control she accepted the parcel, her fingers brushing his briefly as she did.

Josh gave her a short nod. "I'll see you Monday."

Then, in a roar, he was gone. Callie stood and watched his retreating taillights, then turned to let herself inside and locked her door carefully behind her. She rested her head against the door. He'd wanted to kiss her, she was sure of it. Kiss her and more. She was no naive ingénue. She knew desire when she saw it.

So why hadn't he acted on it? Why hadn't he breached the distance between them and taken her mouth with his? Her lips had burned under the touch of his stare, burned for the reality and not the dream.

Callie straightened up from the door and forced herself to pull her thoughts, and her hormones, under control. She stepped through into her sitting room off the small hallway and dropped her evening bag on the coffee table. Then, carefully, she laid the package on the sofa. Her fingers were uncharacteristically clumsy as she plucked at the tape securing the package until, finally, she pulled away the paper.

Callie pushed her fisted hand to her mouth to stem the cry of recognition as the painting was finally revealed.

"*Hope*."

He'd given her *Hope*.

Four

Saturday morning dawned with a hint of rain on the horizon. Already the air outside was warming and the weather promised to be hot and sticky with the coming showers. What she wouldn't give for a lead-up to Christmas in a cooler climate for a change. Callie padded down the stairs and walked through to her kitchen, automatically switching on the jug for the mandatory cup of Earl Grey tea that drove the sluggishness of sleep from her body each morning.

Well, it would, had she been able to sleep. When she hadn't been tangled in her sheets, tossing and turning, her dreams had been fractured by overtones of the night before. Of the sensation of Josh Tremont's hand on her back, of the scent of his subtle cologne in the confines of his car. Of the heat of his gaze before he'd left her at the front door and of her own body's insistent response.

Every workday for the past two weeks she'd managed to keep a lid on her reaction to him. And then he had to go and mess that all up by insisting she accompany him to the gallery.

Unexpected anger rose swiftly from the pit of her stomach. He'd gone too far giving her the painting last night. No matter how much she'd wanted it, a person just didn't do things like that—at least not in her world. In her world every gain had its price. Some you could afford, some you couldn't, and this was very definitely one she couldn't afford on any level.

As she waited for the pot of tea to draw she stomped through to her sitting room and stopped to stare at the painting she'd left propped up on the seat of her cream leather two-seater. Her chest constricted as her eyes locked on the figure.

It was impossible. No, Josh Tremont was impossible. There was no way she could accept this gift from him. She'd return it to him today. Monday would be too late. If she held on to it a moment longer than necessary she might just give in and keep it and there was no way her pride would allow her to do that. She was already in over her head repaying a debt she'd never asked for. She certainly didn't want to owe Josh as well.

She flung a glare at the mantel clock that ticked quietly

in the background. Was seven-thirty too early to call your boss on a Saturday morning? With a huff of air through pursed lips, she conceded that any time before Monday was probably too early.

Nine. She'd phone him at nine on the dot and sort out some time to drop it back to him.

Decision made, her head finally felt clearer. She could almost enjoy her low-fat cereal and milk, sweetened with a scattering of dried apricots. Almost. By the time the clock had ticked slowly to nine she had already showered, dressed, stripped her bed and remade it, and her first load of laundry was nearly ready to be hung on the line.

The machine beeped discreetly from the annexe in her garage, letting her know the cycle was finished just as she picked up her phone and punched in Josh's home number.

The repetitive burr-burr of the ringtone was almost hypnotic. Clearly he wasn't home, but didn't he have staff, or even an answering machine? She was on the verge of hanging up when the phone was picked up.

"Tremont."

The two syllables hammered down the phone with no-nonsense decisiveness.

"It's Callie."

Suddenly the tone in his voice changed to the warm texture of liquid honey. "Ah, Callie. Give me a minute, I've just got out the pool and I'm dripping everywhere."

She heard the receiver clatter to a hard surface and a rustle of fabric. While she waited, her mind went into overdrive, imagining how Josh would look sleek and wet and straight from the pool. His dark hair would be slicked back, exposing the broad strong plane of his forehead and rivulets of water would track down the corded strength of his neck and over his powerful shoulders. She threw the brakes on her thoughts before her imagination went any further.

There was a faint scraping sound through the earpiece and then his voice filled her ear again.

"How are you this morning?"

"I'm fine. Look, I should get right to the point. I really appreciate what you did with the painting last night but I can't accept it."

"Why is that, Callie?" Her name rippled through the handset of her phone in his rich, deep voice, sending a stroke of something forbidden down the back of her neck. "I thought you liked the picture."

"I do, it's just…"

"Just?" he prompted.

How did you tell your employer that such a gift was inappropriate without putting his nose out of joint? Especially since she had to inveigle herself into his world more effectively than she had already done if she was to garner any of the information Irene would no doubt be pumping her for soon.

So far Josh had appeared to be exactly what the world expected. Charming, successful, driven—a man who gave 100 percent at all times and expected the same in return. As an employer, Callie couldn't fault him. In fact, she'd almost begun to wonder if he wasn't just particularly gifted at reading the market and hadn't had to resort to corporate espionage to undermine the Palmers.

Josh continued. "You have a strong connection with the picture. Am I wrong?"

Callie drew in a sharp breath at his acuity. "No, you weren't wrong."

"Then it's yours."

"No. It's worth far too much."

"And if I think you're worth that, and more?"

"I—" She faltered.

"Don't make a big deal of it, Callie. You liked the painting, I bid on it on your behalf and my bid won."

He made it sound so simple. She liked the painting, *connected* to it, therefore it was hers. The fact that the price tag had probably run into five figures had nothing to do with it. Her mind scrambled for logic, suddenly latching on to his very words to give her valid cause to return the picture to him.

"No," she said firmly. "I can't accept it. I do identify with the painting, perhaps a bit too much."

"It upsets you?"

"Yes," she lied, catching her lower lip between her teeth and biting hard before she changed her mind.

"I'm sorry. That wasn't my intention."

"I know," she hurried to say. "And I appreciate the gesture, really, I do. But I'd like to return it to you. Today if possible."

He didn't answer at first, then she heard a soft exhalation. "Dinner, my place, six-thirty."

"But—"

Dinner? With her boss? At his home?

"I'll see you then. Don't dress up."

The rapid-fire beeps indicating a disconnected tone signalled that he'd ended the call. Did she really have to go? Callie replaced her handset in its charging station and walked to the sitting room. Her eyes fixed on the painting. If she really meant to give it back, she would have to.

Callie alighted from her parked car and tucked the rewrapped package firmly under one arm. He'd said not to dress up, but she'd felt the need to make some effort. The floating hand-painted silk panels of her pale emerald sundress swirled around her legs as her feet, clad for once in flats, marched toward Josh's front door.

When she'd arrived at the entrance to his driveway she'd almost chickened out, telling herself she should have waited until Monday. But, she had to admit, his summons for dinner gave her the perfect opportunity to observe him in a different setting—and she needed to find some grounding in her observations very soon.

The driveway to the mansion was imposing enough with its boxed hedging trimmed to immaculate precision, but the house itself was something else entirely. The twin-arched portico of his home stood austerely before her and an entire squadron of butterflies went into battle formation in her stomach.

Everything was so incredibly perfect. Not a line or even so much as a leaf out of place. He must have a whole fleet of gardeners keeping it all so pristine.

"Are you going to stand out there all day enjoying the garden or did you want to come inside?"

Callie jumped. She hadn't even heard the front door swing open. She gave Josh a half smile.

"Your gardens are very…" She faltered. "Beautiful," she finally said.

It was the truth, they were beautiful. But despite their perfection she missed the exuberance of colour and shape she was used to seeing in a spring garden. These precisely clipped hedges and trees lacked something.

Soul. That was it. While there was growth in abundance, there was no life in what she saw. It was as though everything was about appearances and not about personal pleasure.

"But you don't like them, do you?" Josh leaned against one of the cream-coloured pillars supporting the arches at his front door.

"It's not that," Callie said carefully. "They are lovely, just a little too controlled for my liking."

"And you prefer things more uncontrolled?"

There was a wealth of innuendo in Josh's tone and Callie felt a flush of warmth rise up her throat and spread through her cheeks. Heavens, she hadn't blushed in years!

"When there's a time and place for it, yes."

Callie lifted her chin and met his gaze full on. His eyes gleamed with humour. He knew he'd embarrassed her with his teasing and he was enjoying it.

It was a side of him she hadn't seen before. In the office he was driven professionalism all the way. She found it interesting that her first impression, of the outside of his home at least, was exactly the same. A place for everything and everything in its place.

Yet, as something deep inside her unfurled under his amused gaze, she knew much more lay beneath the surface.

"Come inside," Josh said as he pushed off from the pillar and gestured to the door. "We can have a drink by the pool before dinner."

Callie took the few steps necessary to close the distance between them and slid the wrapped painting out from under her arm.

"Here, this is yours."

Josh reached to take the package from her, but paused for a moment before accepting it.

"Are you sure?"

"Definitely."

He gave a small nod and accepted the packet. Then, with his hand settled on the small of her back as he had done last night, he guided her inside his home.

Callie tried to ignore his closeness and the heated imprint of his hand through the silk of her dress, but it was nearly impossible. Every nerve ending concentrated on that one spot. On the outline of his fingers, on the warmth of his palm. She let go the breath she hadn't even realised she was holding when he stepped away from her to shut the door.

Dressed casually, he was no less imposing than he was in his standard office attire. He still favoured dark colours, the navy polo shirt hanging loose over jeans whose cut and style screamed designer chic. He wore no cologne today, but his intrinsic male scent still put every hormone in Callie's body on full alert.

What was she thinking? She was supposed to be spying on the man, not lusting for him.

Josh placed the picture on a sideboard, then continued to guide Callie outdoors to the pool area. As they exited the wide-open French doors to the back of the house, he removed his hand from her back and let her move forward a step or two away from him. She had her hair up again and he found his eyes riveted to the smooth straight line of her neck. A tiny curl had escaped at the edge of her hairline and caressed her nape. His fingers itched to gently wind the tiny strand of hair around them, to see if his touch would cause a shiver to run over her skin.

She walked with a grace that was hard to ignore. The fabric of her dress skimming over the curve of her hips and swaying gently with the totally female movement of her legs as they crossed the tiled expanse of floor. He wondered, not for the first time, if her movements would be as graceful in the bedroom.

Something deep inside him tightened and a flare of heat blossomed at its nucleus. He looked forward to finding out. It would be a pleasure for them both.

"What would you like to drink?" he asked as he held out a cushion-covered, wrought-iron chair for her to sit down on.

"Something cool and nonalcoholic, please."

Josh was a little surprised. "Sure you don't want a glass of wine?"

"No, thanks. I never drink alcohol when I'm driving."

"Wise choice. Fruit punch okay?"

"Sounds delicious."

He watched the muscles in the slender line of her throat move as she swallowed imperceptibly. She was nervous. Intriguing. In the office she worked at his side with impeccable efficiency—even last night she'd been the same, despite her obvious annoyance at him taking it for granted that she'd be there with him.

Was it the idea of having returned the painting that made her feel this way, he wondered. Returning a gift was never a particularly easy thing to do. He knew enough about her circumstances to understand why the message the artist had conveyed with a series of skilful brushstrokes would have resonated with her. Any teen who'd been through Irene Palmer's system had come from tougher backgrounds than most and Callie was very much the poster child for what Irene's foundations worked to achieve. Reluctantly, he had to hand it to the old bag: she'd got it right with Callie.

Josh reached for a condensation-sweating pitcher on the drinks trolley by their table and poured two glasses of fruit punch.

"Are you driving, too?" Callie asked, with a hint of acerbity, as she accepted her drink.

"No, but I don't need alcohol to have a good time."

His words seemed to relax her and her features settled into a smile.

The investigation he'd made into her past was scant on details but he knew, from the confidential file his staff had compiled, that there'd been family problems with drug and alcohol dependency. She'd chosen to walk—or, more precisely, run—away from it, losing herself in the streets of Auckland's inner city. And despite that, she'd survived. He admired her all the more for making a personal stand when it came to her own choices.

Over their dinner of succulent eye-fillet steaks, baby potatoes and sliced zucchini and capsicum seared on the barbecue, it amused him to have Callie probe carefully about his own past.

"So you were brought up by your mother?" Callie asked.

"Yeah, I was. We lived in Wellington."

"She must be proud of you."

"She's dead," he answered bluntly.

"Oh, I'm so sorry. I didn't know. You must miss her very much." Genuine remorse filled Callie's eyes.

"Every single day. She died far too young." Josh didn't even try to keep the bitterness from his voice.

"You were lucky to have always had her support, though. That kind of thing can never be taken for granted."

There was a wistfulness in Callie's voice that pulled him very much into the present.

"You're right. Sometimes I just need to be reminded of that fact." Josh forced himself to smile at Callie. "And she would have been proud of me. It was always her greatest wish to see me succeed."

A light sea breeze wafted across the air, bringing a cool change to the evening.

"Come on, let's go inside for dessert and coffee. It's getting cold."

Callie started to pick up the plates from the table. Josh put his hand firmly over hers and drew it to his chest.

"Uh-uh. You're not here to work. I can take care of them later."

With a faint nod of acquiescence, she allowed him to draw her away from the table and up the shallow tiled stairs, between tall cypresses, that led toward the back of the house.

Over homemade shortcake, courtesy of his day housekeeper, and the decaf coffee Callie insisted on, Josh maintained very general conversation, but he wasn't oblivious to the way Callie's eyes darted around the room from time to time. Especially when her gaze alighted, with barely concealed interest, on a collection of framed photographs on the sideboard.

"Do you mind?" she asked, gesturing to the pictures.

"Sure, why not?"

He followed her over to the pictures. She unerringly picked up the duplicate of the one he had in his office.

"This is you and your mum, isn't it? It's the same as the one at work." She smiled, her fingertip tracing the outline of his youthful face behind glass. "You both look so happy."

"She was still well then and, yes, despite everything, we were happy," Josh conceded.

"I'm glad," Callie said simply. She shot a look at her wristwatch. "Oh, is that the time? I must head off. I've really enjoyed this evening. Thank you."

As he saw her to the door he knew he needed to make his first definitive move.

"I hope you weren't too upset that I couldn't keep the painting," Callie said as she pressed the button on her key to unlock her car.

"Not upset exactly," Josh responded, choosing his words carefully.

"Oh?"

"Just sorry I caused you distress in any way."

As Callie started to speak again Josh placed his index finger firmly against her lips. "Don't make excuses for me. I can handle making a mistake every now and then."

Before she could summon a protest, he lowered his head to hers and replaced his fingertip with his lips. The sudden jolt that shattered through him came as a complete surprise. Yes, logically he knew he found her attractive. What red-blooded hetero guy wouldn't? But the searing heat plunging through his veins was totally unexpected. He fought to not pull her to him, to align the soft curves of her body against the hard planes of his. To answer the primitive roar that filled his mind even as he fought to keep the kiss light.

She tasted of the mixed berries and white chocolate shortcake, and the sweetness, combined with her own unique flavour, spread through his senses like an intoxicating elixir.

Not touching her was torment. Taking her lips not enough. With a groan, he gave in to his body's demands and slid his arms around her, gathering her to him. The smooth fabric of her dress slithered against his palms as he stroked across her back. Beneath the silky fabric he felt the heat of her skin and instantly wanted to know its texture more intimately.

Callie's hands still remained at her side, her fingers clenched around her car keys. He could feel her tension in every line of her body. Gently, he deepened his kiss, sweeping his tongue past her lips to stroke hers, to absorb the tiny sounds she made. Sounds that sent his blood pulsing even faster and hotter through his veins.

A small tremor undulated through her body—if he hadn't been holding her so close he might have missed it—but it signalled her capitulation. Her mouth opened wider, her tongue met his and her keys dropped unheeded to the driveway as she raised her hands and linked them around his neck, pulling him closer to her.

Her breasts pressed now against his chest, her hips aligned with his, her mound pressing against the rigid length of his desire for her. There was no hiding it. He was unequivocally aroused.

The realisation of how close he was to losing control sluiced through his mind with the effectiveness of a bucket of iced water. He didn't want to rush this.

Slowly, Josh withdraw from their embrace, but the insistent hammer of his heart in his chest belied the call his mind had just made. He trailed a line of small kisses from the corner of Callie's mouth and up the soft curve of her cheekbone until his lips rested against her temple.

Her breath came in short, sharp puffs of air against the bare skin at the opening of his shirt. His imagination flew into overdrive wondering what it would be like to feel her breath over the rest of his body. He bit back a curse and summoned every ounce of control he had left.

Josh lifted his hands to frame Callie's face and tilted her head slightly, forcing her to meet his gaze.

"I'm glad you came over tonight."

"I…" Her voice foundered with confusion.

"You know I want to see you again." He kissed her slightly parted lips once last time. "And I'm not just talking about in the office."

"I…I don't know."

"Worried what people will say? We can keep it quiet for now if you want. Think about it, okay?"

He bent and retrieved her car keys from the driveway and opened the car door for her.

"Promise me you'll drive home safely," he said, his eyes boring into hers.

"I will."

Confusion reflected in her eyes. He'd wager tonight hadn't been what she'd anticipated at all. For him it had been an unexpected bonus.

"See you Monday. We'll talk more then."

"Yes, Monday."

She was operating on autopilot now, and the realisation gave him a sense of supreme male satisfaction. Obviously, their kiss had rattled her as much as it had him.

Callie took her keys from his outstretched hand, her fingertips tingling as they brushed against his palm. She still couldn't quite believe that he'd kissed her, nor could she rationalise her overwhelming reaction to that kiss. Somehow she had to pull herself together and get herself home. From hidden reserves of strength she dragged up the automatic behaviour required to clip on her seat belt and start her car.

As she drove up the driveway, she stole a look in the rearview mirror. Josh stood exactly where she'd left him, bathed in the golden outdoor lighting, a strong silhouette watching her as she drove away. Her breath quickened in her chest as she felt the strength of his perusal through the dark night air and she lifted a hand to her face, her fingertips resting against her lips as if by doing so she could relive his touch all over again.

By the time she got home, she could almost fool herself that she'd pulled her act together. Right up until the moment she got inside and saw the red eye on her answering machine winking at her across the room.

Five

Irene's voice filled the air with the modulated tones that gave witness to her impeccable upbringing and her private school education.

"Callie, it's been two weeks. Call me in the morning. Surely you have something for me."

Callie hit the erase key, but it did nothing to clear the frustration that still hung in the air with a palpable presence. Something for Irene? She had nothing. Absolutely nothing, except a growing sense of admiration for a man she should not have allowed to kiss her tonight.

Of course he was ruthless. Look at where he'd come from, what he'd achieved on his own. Was it possible that the Palmers had it all wrong and that it was merely strong business acumen that kept Josh one step ahead of them on so many contracts lately? As far as poaching staff went, that kind of thing happened everywhere. Of course he wanted to surround himself with the best of the best. It was no less than what he offered himself.

Her inner muscles clenched tight as she thought of what he'd offered her tonight. Of the promise inherent in his kiss, the impression of his hard body against hers and of his statement that he wanted to "see" her again.

Callie flopped down on a nearby chair, not even bothering to switch on a light. It was crazy. She'd gone to work for Josh Tremont bent on discovering where he had his inside track on the Palmers' business plans and now she was doing what she never dreamed she'd allow herself to do. She was falling for him.

Day by day a little harder, week by week a little deeper. What had started out as merely a physical attraction was rapidly turning into something more. Something she wanted to explore without the sense that their interaction was something that should be totally forbidden.

She was there purely at Irene's behest, she reminded herself, to do what she could to save Palmer Enterprises from further losses. Not to do anything as foolish as falling in love.

Oh, no, surely not love. She didn't even know what that was. Her upbringing, for want of a better word, had made up in abuse for what it had lacked in care and attention. For self-preservation she'd fled as soon as she'd turned fourteen, relying on her wits and a well-honed instinct to survive to keep her safe on the streets for two years until an error in judgement had seen social services and the police finally catch up with her.

She'd initially fought placement in one of Irene Palmer's foster homes, but after realising that no matter how many times she ran away they were always going to bring her back, she decided to accept what they offered.

That chance to turn her life around and make better choices had been a rebirth in more ways than one. But Callie had always been careful not to trust too deeply and not to like anyone too much. Relationships with others were surface only, never deep. Her world had always been on ground that was too shaky for that.

No, she couldn't be falling in love with Josh. It was too crazy for words. But nobody said she couldn't enjoy this for what it was worth. She was a normal, healthy woman with normal, healthy appetites. And maybe, just maybe, she could prove the Palmers' fears wrong about Josh.

Monday morning Callie was instantly aware of the deep sense of emptiness in the office when she arrived. Usually Josh was at his desk a good hour or more before she arrived, but today his absence was a physical thing.

She'd no sooner reached her desk than her phone started to ring.

"Callie, I'll be working from home today and I need you to access my computer and e-mail some files to me."

Surprised that he didn't have a link from his home

computer to the office, Callie quickly jotted down the file names that Josh rattled off onto her notepad.

"Is there anything else?" she asked, determined to keep the same level of professionalism as he obviously exhibited.

"Yeah," his voice dropped an octave. "I can't wait to see you again, but it'll have to wait until I get back from Sydney."

"Sydney?" Callie refused to acknowledge the surge of pleasure his words had sent through her.

"Unexpected trip. I've already organised the jet and I'll be leaving in a couple of hours for the airport."

"I'll reschedule your appointments. When do you anticipate being back?"

"All going well, tomorrow, maybe Wednesday afternoon at the latest."

Callie ran her eye over his electronic diary, mentally shifting his appointments to ensure the least disruption. "Okay, that should be fine."

"Good. Will you miss me?"

Her breath caught on a soft gasp. Of course she'd miss him, but she couldn't admit that.

"It'll give me a chance to catch up a bit," she hedged.

Josh laughed, the sound sending a tingle of longing from her ear to her core. "You can admit it, you know."

"Admit what?" Callie remained deliberately vague.

"That you're looking forward to seeing me again. How about dinner on Wednesday night? We'll go somewhere private and intimate. Would you like that?"

Callie hesitated before answering. Of course she'd

like that. In fact, she couldn't wait. The realisation that she'd be alone in the office for the next couple of days was tinged with disappointment already.

"Yes, I would like that. Shall I make a reservation somewhere?" she replied, her voice uncharacteristically husky.

"I'll take care of it," he answered, again in that low tone that made his statement all the more intimate. As if he was going to take care of a great deal more than a simple dinner booking.

Desire simmered through her veins in gentle waves and she shifted on her ever-so-sensible office chair in a way that lacked prudence altogether.

Wednesday. Two days, two nights. It was an eternity and yet so close. The anticipation of his return was going to have her at fever pitch and he knew it. That simple fact alone should have her changing her mind, refusing his invitation, but she wanted more. She wanted him.

"I'll get onto those files for you. Can I access them with my fingerprint and password?"

"I've already spoken to Drew about your print ID on my station, but you'll need my password," Josh said, before rattling off the access letter and number combination she'd need.

He trusted her enough to give her his private password. A swell of joy hit her. Hard on its heels, though, came the diminishing reality of what she could find out with that information and, more particularly, what Irene would *expect* her to find out.

Callie pushed the thought from her head. She'd been

entrusted with this key, she didn't dare abuse that trust. Not when her every instinct told her that Josh Tremont was far more than what everyone else suspected. Not when her heart urged her to obey instinct over rationality for the first time in her life.

As soon as Josh ended their call, Callie walked through to his office. Settling herself into his chair, she couldn't stifle the strange sensation of warmth that permeated her skin. Everything about this room spoke of the man he was, his presence and personality indelibly stamped in its atmosphere.

She gave herself a quick mental shake and logged in to his computer, using her print scan and the password he'd given her. She held her breath a moment as the system hesitated before opening fully, and then she was in. Free to peruse everything and anything that took her fancy.

The message Irene had left on her phone on Saturday night replayed in her head. Callie had the opportunity, here and now, to put things right and settle the matter once and for all. First, though, she had to send those files through to Josh.

Once that had been done, and she'd received the pingback read receipt she'd requested, Callie debated logging straight back out again. There'd be a record of how long she'd been active on Josh's computer somewhere in the system if anyone bothered to look, but the question was Would they? Obviously, if she logged out and logged back in again it would send up a red flag, even if Josh's password worked for her again. She knew his access codes were changed on a random basis.

Perhaps even after giving her this password, it would be invalid for future use.

This was her first and last opportunity. She had to do it, no matter how much it went against her grain. Callie's first loyalty had always been to Irene and she was permitting that loyalty to be compromised by her unexpected emotional response to a man she barely knew.

Taking a deep breath, Callie allowed her fingers to dash over the keyboard, executing a variety of searches using specific keywords. In no time at all she had a list of files and one by one she copied them onto a flash drive so she could study them at home. Silently she vowed to destroy the information as soon as she knew Josh was innocent of what the Palmers accused him of.

For some reason, when she got home, she was reluctant to turn on her computer. Eventually, though, after she'd had a light bite to eat and had brewed a pot of herbal tea, she opened her laptop and powered it up.

A sense of foreboding manifested in a burning sensation in the pit of her stomach as she slotted the memory stick into its spot. A burning sensation that grew stronger as she opened each file she'd copied and skimmed its contents. Josh Tremont seemed to have an awful lot of information about the corporate structure and current business plan at Palmer Enterprises for someone who didn't work there.

On top of that, he had a massive file on Bruce Palmer, detailing everything publicly known about the man, plus a great deal not generally known about him, either. The amassed information bordered on obsessive—certainly far more than one would expect from a business rival, no matter how competitive he was.

Callie sat back in her chair, her hands clenched into fists in her lap. From his notes his intentions were quite clear. He wanted to destroy Palmer Enterprises. But it didn't make sense. Sure, they competed in a healthy marketplace for similar work, and in business it was every man for himself, but why was he so hell-bent on bringing Palmer Enterprises to its corporate knees? This appeared to go much deeper than mere competitiveness. There was something almost chilling in Josh's systematic approach. As if he'd declared war and was working to a strategy that, once implemented, would not stop until his goal was reached.

Callie took a sip of her rapidly cooling tea, hoping the soothing brew would calm the anxiety that had now formed a tight knot in her chest.

For all intents and purposes, the man she had grown so attracted to was not the person he appeared to be at all. Sure, the Josh she knew was focussed, hardworking and driven. But he was also warm and interesting and there was something she glimpsed deep inside him that drew her in ways she'd never encountered with another person before. There was a hurt hidden behind the urbane exterior he presented to the world. A hurt that spoke to something in her heart and urged her to help him heal in any way she could.

Callie closed the windows she'd had open on her computer and was about to shut down when she noticed one file she hadn't opened yet. Its title was innocuous—nothing to even indicate why she'd downloaded it—but she'd searched for files that had the word *Palmer* in them and this one had cropped up.

She double-clicked on the document icon and waited for the file to open.

Her eyes scanned across her screen double-time as she scrolled through the many pages of the Word file. A buzz of excitement thrilled through her veins. This was definitely something big. Something that Tremont Corporation had in place to pre-empt Palmers with an innovative new contract overseas. It would leave Palmers in the corporate dust.

While it wasn't what Irene had specifically asked her to look out for, Callie's mind spun on the possibilities. If Palmers had this information, they would lead the world. And if Josh really was intent on bringing Palmers down, getting ahead of him in this work would stop him as effectively as a heart attack.

The next morning Callie phoned Irene before she left for the office, arranging to meet with her at the older woman's favourite café on the waterfront for lunch.

"I investigated the original author of some of the documents. They didn't try to hide their tracks very well." Callie mentioned the name of one of Bruce's up-and-coming business interns.

"Bruce isn't going to like that, but don't worry. We'll deal with him. He'll be sorry he sold us out."

For a moment Irene looked furious, but then she re-composed herself.

"Everything I found is on here," Callie said, passing the memory stick over the table.

A pang of guilt for what she was doing struck her square in the chest, but, she rationalised, it was no more than Josh had done to them. She'd allowed herself to begin to think he was a different breed from the man Irene had warned her about, which only served to show how cleverly persuasive he really was.

"That's everything?"

"Yes, everything I could find. Seriously, I was shocked when I saw how much information he'd gathered on your family, particularly Bruce. Surely that's not the norm when someone is trying to undermine another firm?"

"Not unless he was looking for dirt to dig up."

"Well, he certainly didn't find any in that lot," Callie said staunchly.

Irene slipped the memory stick into her handbag, a worried frown bisecting her brows.

"There's still something about the man that concerns me. He's a constant threat to us and I want to know why." Irene reached across the table, her perfectly manicured hand now curled like a manacle around Callie's wrist. "You're going to have to get closer to him. Really close. The information you need to get isn't going to be something he keeps on a hard drive anywhere. It'll be something he keeps inside *him.*"

There was an iron command in Irene's voice and Callie shot her a worried glance.

"I mean it, Callie. You've come this far; you're going to have to take it all the way. It's the only chance we have to find out what on earth is behind it all."

All the way? While her mind rejected the idea of allowing herself to be used so clinically, her heart and her pulse rate both leaped at the idea.

"I'll do my best, Irene," Callie said, laying her other hand over the older woman's. "I promise."

Callie was on tenterhooks Wednesday as she waited for Josh's call to announce his arrival back in the country. She'd worked hard all day, trying to distract her thoughts, and her rampant hormones, from the prospect of seeing him again.

She'd just returned from the central library, where she'd delivered some archive material she'd finished with, when she became aware of a change in the air. A level of energy and intensity the office had been lacking while he'd been gone. Had he returned in the short time she'd been away from her desk?

"Callie? Come through to my office, would you?"

He was back. Callie smoothed the form-fitting sleeveless cream turtleneck dress she wore over her hips and walked through to Josh's office. Looking at her, no one would guess how her blood thrummed through her veins or how her nerve endings had suddenly become infinitely attuned to his presence.

She'd no sooner stepped through his door than strong arms wrapped around her body and drew her hard against him. She caught a glimpse of sapphire-blue glitter before his eyes closed and his mouth slanted across hers.

Instantly she parted her lips, giving him free access, allowing him to plunder the soft recess with a hungry sweep of his tongue. Callie reached her hands up around his neck and laced her fingers together, relishing the feel of his hardness against her body, savouring the taste of him on her tongue.

It had only been a matter of days since he'd last kissed her, but it felt like an eon.

When Josh gently withdrew his lips from hers she wanted to protest, but she held back the sound of dismay that gathered in her throat. Men like Josh Tremont did the chasing. It was up to her to allow herself to be caught.

"I didn't imagine it," he said, his voice deep and his breathing a little unsteady.

"Imagine it?"

"How it felt to hold you in my arms. How you respond to me."

Josh brushed the knuckles of one hand over the hardened tips of her breasts, now clearly defined through the stretch knit of her dress. Callie made a mental note to wear padded bras in the office in future.

"And was it as good as you remember?" she teased, a smile curving her lips.

"Better," Josh replied with an answering smile that sent a bolt of electricity sizzling to her core. "You still okay for tonight?"

"Definitely," Callie answered. On more levels than just the one he anticipated, she reminded herself quietly.

"Good. I'll pick you up from your place at six. We'll dine early."

"And then?" she asked, her eyes locked with his in a silent challenge.

"That's entirely up to you."

Six

The balance of the day raced past as Josh worked to get up-to-date on the time he'd missed in the office. He fired commands at Callie like an army general and she earned every cent of her high-priced salary before she finally gathered her things and headed for home.

Heady anticipation saw her race through a shower and, once it was dry, twist her hair up in a loose knot on top of her head. Even as she reapplied her makeup, tendrils glided down to frame her face. She shivered a little at each tiny caress, wondering what it would be like to feel Josh's lips, or the trace of his fingers, along her neck.

She studied her reflection in the mirror. Already her

cheeks carried the soft flush of desire and her eyes gleamed with a need she'd always been able to keep firmly under control before.

A quick glance at her bedside clock reminded her to get her act together and stop daydreaming. She quickly slipped on a pair of black lace panties. The tiny diamantés, sprinkled on the lace, flashed in the overhead light, bringing a smile to her lips. Always a magpie, one way or another, she conceded. After so many years of deprivation Callie unashamedly loved pretty things.

And when it came to pretty, she considered long and hard about the dress she was going to wear tonight. Unsure of where Josh was taking her for their meal, she chose a black halter-neck dress with a chiffon overlayer that floated to just above her knees. The deep V neckline made it impossible to wear a bra and as she gathered the ties into a knot at her nape, she wondered if she should have chosen something a little less obvious.

The summons of her doorbell made that thought redundant. She had no time to change now. She slid her feet into black-and-silver Prada sandals and raced from her room.

Callie's heart hammered in her chest as she opened the door. Her hungry eyes consumed him as Josh filled the entrance. He was dressed all in black, from the handmade loafers on his feet to the open-necked shirt that clung to his broad shoulders like a lover's caress.

Callie stopped herself before she actually licked her lips, but, oh boy, he was delectable.

"Would you like to come in for a drink before we head out?" she asked.

There was something different about him tonight. An edge to his self-control she hadn't sensed before. Concern plucked at the fringes of her mind. Had he discovered that she'd accessed more than the data he'd requested on his computer? She discounted the thought even as it occurred to her. Josh Tremont wasn't the kind of man to let something like that slide. He'd have reamed her out about it if he knew—she was sure of it.

No, it had to be something else. Maybe, she wondered, he was just as tense with anticipation about tonight as she was. They were adults, after all. They'd acknowledged a strong attraction between each other and goodness knew they just about ignited when they kissed.

Callie felt an involuntary tug deep inside at the prospect of going further than just a kiss with Josh. Arousal spread with a flood of heat through her body, and her unfettered breasts tautened, abrading against the fine fabric of her halter with excruciating awareness. She felt his eyes coast over her from the tip of her shoes to the top of her head. Finally, he replied, his voice taut with restraint.

"I don't think so. With the way you look right now, I doubt we'd make it to dinner."

Callie's breath caught on her response. What could she say in the face of that? She lifted her chin and summoned what she hoped was a casual smile. "Another time perhaps."

She locked her front door and walked beside him to the waiting Maserati at the kerbside, not touching but painfully aware of his proximity, of his strength.

"Do we have far to go?" she asked as they started off down the street.

"To the waterfront."

"Oh, anywhere I know?" she probed.

"You'll have to wait and see," came the enigmatic response.

Callie settled back against the soft leather of the car seat and tried to concentrate on the soft rock playing on the CD player, but all her senses remained attuned to the man beside her. She wondered why they were even going through the motions of dinner when it was clear where they would end up. Still, she supposed, going to dinner put a civilised veneer on what was a distinctly uncivilised need currently pumping through her body.

She was surprised when, rather than heading along the bays, Josh turned the car toward the helipad at Mechanics Bay. Once he'd parked the car, he took her by the hand and led her to a waiting helicopter.

The pilot made sure that they were both strapped in and had their headsets on before taking off. Callie's stomach lurched as they flew across the harbour.

"Where are we going?" she asked Josh.

"Are you always this impatient for details?" he replied through the headset.

"Curious, not impatient," she corrected.

Josh merely smiled and nodded his head toward the window. "Satisfied?"

Callie looked past him to the massive white luxury launch floating on the harbour, a large *H* emblazoned on part of its deck.

"We're eating on the boat?"

"I hope you don't get seasick," Josh teased.

"Are you planning to hit the high seas?" Callie answered in kind, even as her hands took a white-knuckled grip on her seat as the helicopter descended.

"Just a leisurely cruise around the harbour while we enjoy our meal, then back to Westhaven."

"Westhaven Marina? But what about your car?"

"I won't be driving. A car will meet us there and take us home later. Don't worry. It's all organised. You know, you're not the only one with a knack for getting things done."

They alighted from the chopper and Callie was relieved to set her feet firmly onto the boat's upper deck. Only now did she get a full appreciation of just how large the vessel was. It had to be over a hundred feet long.

"This isn't yours, is it?" she asked as they made their way down a gently curved staircase to the main deck.

"No, I just borrow it from time to time."

For a moment Callie felt a pang of envy for the other women he might have brought here "from time to time," but then she scolded herself for being so silly. He was a man of the world—a darn fine man of the world at that. There'd be women in his past, probably many of them. But she was the one with him now, and she'd take whatever she could get while it lasted because once he discovered the truth about her working for him—and she had no doubt that he eventually would—memories of nights like tonight would be all she'd have left.

The evening was perfect. With daylight savings time in effect, the early evening light dappled over the calm sea in a glittering caress. In the distance a flock of birds still worked the waters and dotted all over the harbour were pleasure craft under sail or motor. Muted strains of classical guitar danced on the air through a hidden sound system and Callie felt herself sink into the luxury of the setting with a completeness that felt, for once, totally right.

A uniformed steward stood near a carved wooden bar and deftly popped the cork on a chilled bottle of champagne as they arrived on the main deck.

"I took the liberty of ordering some champagne. You're not driving anywhere tonight." Josh spoke softly in her ear, the low pitch sending a hum through her body.

"Thank you. I don't believe I've tried this brand before."

"Then you're in for a delight."

Josh took the two glasses from the steward who melted away into the cabin interior, leaving the two of them alone on the main deck. He handed Callie one glass and gently tapped his cut-crystal flute against hers.

"To getting to know one another better," he said, the simplicity of his words belying their subtext.

"To getting to know you," Callie responded and tipped her glass to take a sip of the golden liquid.

He was right. It was a delight to taste and the gentle fizz in her mouth mirrored the bubbling sensation of lightness that suffused her body. She was glad she'd dressed up for this evening. The fittings and accoutrements surrounding them on this massive statement of luxury and wealth deserved no less.

As she lifted her hand to take another sip of the champagne, the fabric of her gown gently grazed her nipples, sending a shock of awareness through her again. She'd never felt so conscious of her body before, nor so attuned to her companion. Although, truth be told, from the minute she'd set eyes on Josh Tremont, even knowing what he was purportedly capable of, he'd attracted her on a level that was purely instinctive.

Josh gestured toward the curved leather seats arranged at a low coffee table, fixed to the deck.

"Would you like to sit down?"

In response, Callie walked across to the chairs, conscious with every step of Josh only a few centimetres behind her. She could feel the heat of his body like a wall against her back, even though he didn't touch her.

The steward returned with a silver tray with artfully arranged canapés displayed on it.

"Just leave them on the table," Josh instructed.

"Certainly, sir. The chef asked me to let you know your main meal will be ready in half an hour."

"Thank you. That'll be all for now."

With a small respectful bow, the steward withdrew.

Despite the low-pitched purr of the vessel's engines belowdecks, indicating that there had to be others on board, at least to guide it through the waters, Callie felt as if the world had narrowed down to just her and Josh. The sensation made her both nervous and excited at the same time. Desperate to fill the void of conversation between them, she commented on the appetisers before them.

"Here, let me choose for you," Josh said with a smile.

Without waiting for her reply, he lifted a sliver of crostini topped with tiny shrimp in a spread of what looked like cream cheese and chives. Obediently, Callie parted her lips, as he leaned across and slid the morsel between them.

Josh watched as Callie slowly chewed and swallowed. Something hot and tight clenched deep inside him as her tongue swept her lower lip.

"That was delicious," she said, her voice husky.

"Another?" he managed, through a throat that had suddenly grown thick with desire.

His plan had been to woo her tonight. Slowly, deftly, with every sensual weapon in his considerable arsenal, before bringing the evening to its inevitable climax. He would have smiled at the unintentional pun, but all he wanted to do was skip the pleasantries and cut straight to the chase—or, more particularly, the main stateroom that awaited them belowdecks.

He forced himself to clamp a lid on his needs, to slow his reactions to her. To savour every second of this intricate dance. But it proved a great deal more difficult than he had imagined.

"My turn first."

Callie surprised him, taking the initiative, and his advantage from him, as she selected another canapé and held it to his lips. Advantages in human affairs, as in business, could easily be wrested from the inexperienced, he decided, as he took the bite-sized food into his mouth, his lips closing around her forefinger and thumb, and his tongue sliding up to suckle between them.

Her startled gasp broke the heaviness of the air between them as she withdrew her hand and cradled it in her lap. He couldn't have said, later on, what it was that she'd given him to eat but he could describe the expression on her face in intimate detail.

Callie's eyes looked huge, her pupils dilated. A faint hint of colour swiped her cheekbones and mirrored itself on the smooth, slender line of her neck. Beneath the filmy black fabric of her dress, her chest rose and fell, as if she couldn't draw quite enough air into her lungs.

She was the first to break eye contact, and he acknowledged the silent victory with a surge of triumph. Oh, yes, tonight would be spectacular. She was so responsive, so open. In the world in which he lived, such transparency was a novelty, one to be savoured.

There'd be no faking with Callie. He'd know with every sigh, every shudder, every heated flush over her skin, exactly what she was feeling and how much she liked it. The thought was intoxicating, far more so than the excellent champagne.

It was time to turn down the heat a little, though, he

decided and he turned to general conversation to offer
some respite to the cacophony of need that threatened
to derail his legendary cool.

"You were a bit nervous on the flight out. Is flying
a problem for you?" he probed as she took a sip from
her glass.

He watched as she slowly replaced her glass on the
table, noted how the sun gilded the light sheen of moisture
on her lips. So much for turning down the heat. He fought
with the urge to lean across and trace that shimmer with
the tip of his tongue and then to delve into the moist heat
of her mouth and find out how she tasted with the hint of
vintage champagne on her tongue. It would be so easy.

"I've never been a relaxed flyer. No real fear, but just
that sense of not being in control. That unnerves me."

"You don't trust easily?"

Josh reached out and took one of her hands in his,
and lightly stroked his thumb across the inside of her
wrist. Her pulse responded beneath his touch with a
sudden flutter.

"No."

She pulled away from his touch, ostensibly to help
herself to another canapé but he knew it was to distance
herself from his question. And what she didn't say in-
trigued him.

"But you did trust the Palmers?"

Her eyes sharpened. "Why do you ask that?"

"Well, you spent time in one of Irene's homes and
you've worked for them ever since. That implies a
certain level of trust."

"Does that bother you?"

"No, not at all. Do you trust me?"

"Should I?" she hedged, meeting his gaze briefly before her eyes flitted away again.

Josh let one side of his mouth draw up in a half smile. "What's not to trust?"

"What, indeed? Maybe I should ask the same of you? Do you trust me?"

"Would I have hired you if I didn't? Don't worry, Callie, I trust you."

Her eyes flew back to his. Silently he cursed himself for letting the mood of the evening grow too clinical. General conversation was one thing, but right now he preferred the loaded atmosphere that had undulated between them. An atmosphere heavy with promise, one he intended to deliver on.

"Dance with me," he commanded, rising to his feet and offering his hand.

"Is that what's necessary right now?" Callie parried, even as she lay her hand in his.

"Oh, yes, it's absolutely necessary." Josh smiled in return. "What would a beautiful evening, out on the water like this, be if we didn't make the most of every second?"

He drew her close against his body. He was more than semi-aroused, a state he'd grown used to in her proximity, and he wasn't afraid for her to know it. He sensed the moment she recognised his desire for her, and felt her stiffen in his arms before relaxing once more. As their steps moved in perfect synchronicity across the deck, he made sure she understood that this dance was only the beginning of what they would achieve together tonight.

Her breasts brushed against his chest—their movement confirming his suspicion that she wore no bra. It was all he could do to restrain himself from undoing the knot of fabric at her nape and letting the pieces drop to expose her to his sight, his touch.

The light spice of her fragrance teased his nostrils. It was a headier perfume than the one she wore in the office, which was so light it was a mere hint of femininity. But this perfume, it spoke of so much more.

Josh bent his head and inhaled her scent more deeply, letting his lips graze across the curve of her neck where it met her deliciously bare shoulders. Callie trembled at his touch, but he knew it was not in fear. The tips of her breasts hardened against his shirt. The knowledge that only two layers of fabric separated their skin was both a torment and a thrill.

He traced the cord of her neck with the tip of his tongue, punctuating its track with small kisses. Fire roared in his veins as she moaned with pleasure, and he captured the sound with his mouth, his lips closing over hers, his tongue gently caressing the soft membrane within with intimate care.

He was rock hard, his body now trembling with suppressed need. With one kiss she drove him to the brink as no woman had ever done before. He wanted her with a passion that bordered on compulsive. He dragged his lips from her mouth and rested his forehead against hers.

"How hungry are you?" he asked, his voice little more than a growl.

"For dinner?" Callie replied, a tiny hitch in her voice. She shook her head ever so slightly. "Not very."

"For me?"

"Starving."

Seven

With her clamped to his side, Josh made a swift call to the kitchen to demand that dinner be delayed until further notice. Callie knew that on some level she should be embarrassed. He'd all but stated their intentions to the crew as to what they'd be doing, but instead all she could think of was that there would be some relief to the pounding ache that suffused her.

Josh led her through the interior of the boat and down a flight of stairs. At the bottom he turned and let her go only long enough to grip the gleaming brass handles on a pair of polished wooden doors and thrust the doors open.

The stateroom was sumptuous in its appointments. Light spilled in from the windows on either side, giving the impression that they were totally alone, afloat on the Waitemata Harbour in their own cocoon of luxury. Callie felt a thrill of anticipation ripple through her as she surveyed the massive bed sprawled in front of her. A thrill that was rapidly followed by a surge of fear.

What was she thinking? This was craziness personified. She'd worked for Josh two and a half weeks, had only met him once before that, and now she was going to bed with him? She'd never behaved so impulsively, nor wantonly, before. The dichotomy between her careful lifestyle over the past few years and what she was about to do slammed home.

"Josh?" she said, her voice betraying her hesitancy.

"Don't think," he said, taking her into his arms again and lowering his lips to hers. "Just feel."

As he kissed her, she clung to reason for a fleeting second, then was swept away on a tide of want she'd never experienced so deeply before. Every nerve in her body, every thought in her head, focussed on Josh Tremont and the way he touched her.

Broad hands swept across her naked back, his fingers tangling in the trail of the ties of her halter. In seconds she felt the fabric of her dress begin to loosen, in a heartbeat she knew he held each tie in his hands. Josh straightened and looked at her.

"I've been wanting to do this all evening."

Callie laughed softly, the sound unexpected in the taut atmosphere of the room. "So you haven't been wanting to do it long then," she teased.

But then all thought of humour fled as Josh smiled

and lowered his hands, drawing the material in a sensuous slide across her sensitised skin. Breath shuddered through her lips as he bared her to his view, as his eyes darkened to indigo and his jaw clenched, his lips compressed in a straight line.

He said nothing, did absolutely nothing—but look. Uncertainty swept through her until he lifted his hands and gently cupped the pale globes of her breasts, his thumbs skimming the hardened, rose-tinted peaks, his touch drawing a cry of need from her mouth that echoed through her entire body. His fingers tightened more firmly on her and she pressed against his hands, suddenly eager for more.

Josh dipped his head and captured one distended nipple with his lips, nibbling gently at the pebbled tip until Callie thought her legs would buckle and send them both to the lushly carpeted floor.

"You like that," he said, his breath a tantalising caress across the moisture on her skin.

"Oh, yes," she groaned.

"You want more?"

"Please, more!"

As Josh laved her other nipple with the same attention, he found the zippered fastening of her dress. In an instant the fabric slithered down over her hips and down her legs to fall in folds of darkness onto the floor. Josh stepped away from her, his eyes raking over her near nakedness, the impressive bulge in the front of his trousers saying more loudly how she affected him than any word or gesture could.

Despite the fact that she was dressed solely in black lace panties and high-heeled sandals, Callie felt invulnerable. She wasn't the only one lost on this wave of attraction. She wasn't the only one to throw reason to the wind and to want to indulge entirely in sensation.

"One more thing," Josh said, reaching for the clip that bound her hair.

As her locks cascaded down, he swept her up and off her feet, closing the distance between the door and the bed with two long strides. He ripped back the covers with one hand and tumbled her onto the crisp cotton sheets. Callie reached down to remove her sandals.

"Leave them," Josh commanded as he tore at the buttons on his shirt and then unfastened his belt and trousers.

Callie heard the thud of his shoes as he dragged the shirt off his shoulders and pushed his trousers and underwear down in an economy of movement that spoke volumes about his need for her.

And then there he was, gloriously naked, his arousal proudly jutting from a nest of dark hair at his groin. Callie's hands twisted in the sheets as her eyes roamed his body—the taut abdomen, the bunched muscles of his chest. She wanted to touch him. To lick and taste the golden planes of his skin, to cup his manhood in her palm and to stroke the swollen tip until he was near bursting. But Josh clearly had other plans.

He wrapped his fingers around her ankles and eased her legs apart, slowly easing his body between them. His hand skimmed down the length of one leg to the hollow at her groin where he pressed a hot wet kiss before stroking back down her thigh, her calf, until he held her foot in his hand. He bent her knee and hooked her foot around his waist before doing the same to her again on the other side.

This time when he pressed his lips to her skin she thought she'd fly off the bed. Energy coiled in a tight knot at the apex of her thighs, begging for his touch, but still he held himself carefully away from her. She reached for the scrap of lace that lay between her and the freedom his touch promised but Josh grabbed her hands, holding them down at her sides.

"Not yet," he murmured. "They're the only thing keeping me under control right now."

"But what if I don't want control. What if I want you. Now."

Callie lifted her hips in supplication, driven by a longing desperate to be assuaged.

"Like this?" he taunted as he leaned forward, and lowered his hips to hers.

Through her panties she felt the hot, hard length of him. She squirmed against him, locking her ankles together so he couldn't immediately pull away, and relished the pressure of his hardness against her yearning flesh.

"Oh, yes," she sighed.

"Soon. But first…"

Josh kept a firm hold on her hands as he lowered his chest to hers. She felt the solid heat of his body before he allowed himself to brush the tips of her breasts. She fought against his hold. She wanted to wrap her arms around him, to hold him to her, length for length, to absorb his heat, his desire. She strained upwards, her head tilting back, exposing the curve of her throat and he trailed hot sucking kisses along her skin, along the line of her collarbone and, finally, drawing each nipple in turn into his mouth, rolling its hardness with his tongue.

Jolts of electricity pulsed through her with each pull of his mouth. Damn, she was close. She'd never been so close without direct stimulation before. Callie flexed her hips, desperate to reach the pinnacle that loomed just on the horizon, but instead moaned in protest as Josh slowed his assault on her senses and began to work his way back down her body.

Finally, he let go her hands, replacing his hold on her hips instead, tilting her pelvis up. Callie let her legs drop from his waist and fall open. Her hands now gripping his shoulders as he covered her mound with his mouth, blowing hot air through her panties and against her most sensitive place, and just about launching her into orbit at the same time.

It didn't matter what he did, where he touched, she ignited. Every particle in her body attuned to his actions, every sense in synch with his touch. Her mind focussed only on him.

He tugged at her panties, finally pulling them down off her body. Then, painstakingly slowly he took off her sandals, pressing kisses against her instep as he released each foot.

Callie never knew she had so many erogenous zones. One touch, one caress, was all it took and she was burning up. Rendered incapable of any thought other than what came next.

Vaguely, she became aware of Josh grabbing his trousers from the floor, extracting a square packet, before ripping it open and sheathing himself. Then he was back between her legs, his hair tickling her inner thighs as he bent to intimately kiss her. Soft at first, then stronger, punctuated by sweeps of his tongue swirling over the hypersensitive bundle of nerve endings at her core. When he closed his mouth around her protruding bud, and suckled, she swept over the edge of reason and into a wild conflagration—spiralling over and over as paroxysms of pleasure shook her body.

She'd barely begun to regain her senses when she felt the hard nub of his erection at her entrance. She opened for him, welcoming him into her body—into her very soul.

Aftershocks of satisfaction from her orgasm soon built into something stronger as he stroked his length in and out, grinding against her, watching her face as she changed from sated satisfaction to hunger all over again.

This time he built her up more quickly than before. The direct pressure of his body, his long deep strokes, culminating in waves of spreading fulfilment that swelled through her again and again. Every muscle in her body tightened, and she held him to her, pulling him deeper, until she lost complete track of where she ended and he began. And then, when she knew she could hold back the tide no longer, she felt the power surge through him as he climaxed. A raw growl of completion ripped from his throat as he pumped against her over and over, sending her into the true oblivion of sybaritic bliss.

Callie stirred, noting immediately the tightening of Josh's arms around her as they lay sprawled together in abandon across the bed. The sun was lower now, and she could see streaks of purple and rich apricot across the sky through the window.

She lifted one hand to his abdomen and began to stroke, in long languid sweeps, with the tips of her fingers. Beneath her touch she felt goose bumps rise over his skin. She lowered her hand, tracing tiny patterns through the coarse hair at his groin until she reached the smooth length of him. She wrapped her fingers around him, sliding them gently up and down his shaft, squeezing ever so slightly more firmly as she reached his tip before beginning the same journey again.

Josh's eyelids opened to half mast as she stroked him, the cerulean glitter his only betrayal of control. Callie slid down his body and drew up onto her knees.

She bent down and traced his tip with her tongue before opening her mouth to take him fully while keeping up the momentum of her hand on his shaft. Beneath her she felt the muscles in his thighs clench and she took him deeper, increasing her rhythm, relentlessly alternating pressure with her mouth, her tongue.

When he came it was with giant shudders that wracked

his body and shook the bed, in total contrast to the taut control he'd held over his body as she'd ministered to him. And, as the last waves of pleasure washed over him, Callie knew a completion she'd never known before. She'd brought him to this. She'd given him the ultimate satisfaction.

Josh pulled her into his arms, aligning her body over his, his hands stroking lazy circles across her back as she nuzzled against his chest.

"I suppose we should put the chef out of his misery and have dinner," he eventually said.

Callie's stomach growled in response, eliciting a hearty chuckle from Josh.

"That settles it."

He reached a lazy arm out and lifted a phone from the bedside cabinet. His instructions were brief and to the point. They'd serve themselves in the salon on the main deck and they didn't want to be disturbed.

Callie rose from the bed and stretched before reaching for her clothes. Josh came up behind her, his hands arresting her actions.

"Don't bother with those. There are robes in the en suite. I like the idea of sitting opposite you, knowing you're not wearing anything else."

"I wasn't wearing much else before," Callie commented but walked through to the bathroom.

"I know," Josh's voice followed her. "It drove me nuts."

"And this won't?" she answered, stepping back through to the bedroom and tying the sash on a rich emerald satin robe.

The fabric slithered over her skin, its touch triggering tiny ripples of sensation that brought an immediate response and saw her nipples peak in clearly defined outlines. Josh's eyes riveted on them. Unbelievably, she felt them tighten even more.

"Oh, yeah, it'll drive me nuts."

Callie handed him the large black towelling robe she'd chosen for him. "You'd better put this on then. We can torment each other."

She shoved her hands deep into her pockets as Josh pulled on his robe.

"Shall we?" he said, reaching for her hand.

It felt like the most natural thing in the world to have her hand in his. His fingers laced with hers and the warmth of his palm scorched against her skin, fusing them together.

In the main salon an intimate table for two had been set, a fresh bottle of champagne languished in an ice bucket to one side and the subdued lighting was enhanced by a myriad of squat candles scattered about.

By the time they'd dined on smoked salmon filo parcels, drizzled with a sweet chilli sauce, and a medley of seasonal roasted vegetables, Callie was on tenterhooks. The enticing glimpses she caught of Josh's bare chest as he leaned forward at the table distracted her from the flavoursome meal before them, and she was all too aware of the tension building up deep inside.

Tension that saw her shift every so often on her seat to alleviate the insistent throb at the juncture of her thighs. Tension that made her all too aware of the movement of the muscles in Josh's throat as he swallowed. Of the play of veins on his hands as he deftly sectioned his filo parcel and brought each bite to his mouth. He was as methodical in this as he was in everything else he did.

But she knew now exactly what it took to make him lose that fabled control and as the sash on her robe began to slide loose, she made no attempt to halt the gape of fabric.

Dessert was soon forgotten as by mutual assent they rose from the table. The distance between the main deck and their room passed in a blur of motion as their appetites for one another coalesced into a melding of bodies, sensation and gratification.

They were ensconced in the private confines of the back of a limousine, fingers still entwined. It was as if, having had a taste of one another, neither could bear to break the link between them. It was past midnight and while she was physically exhausted, Callie had never felt more mentally energised before.

They'd ended their harbour cruise standing by the aft railing on the main deck, Josh's arms wrapped around her from behind, her body fully supported by his strength. There was a bitter sweetness to the knowledge that the evening was drawing to a close, but even perfection had its boundaries. Their return to reality was as reluctant as it was necessary.

As Josh had said, a car was waiting for them at the Westhaven Marina as the boat drew in. Now that car was headed to Callie's town house.

"Stay with me this weekend."

The rumble of Josh's voice in the gloom of the car interior surprised her.

"You want me to stay at your place?"

Her heart leaped at the opportunity, but her head urged caution.

"You don't want to?"

"I didn't say that."

"Good, it's settled then. You can leave your car at work on Friday and we'll drive home together."

"Won't people notice?"

"Does that bother you?" Josh lifted her hand to his lips and drew her forefinger into his mouth. "I want more than just mind-blowing sex from you, Callie."

She gasped as his lips closed around the tip and the wet warmth of his tongue stroked against her skin.

"Wouldn't you like to explore this further?" he coaxed.

"Y-yes."

A shudder ran through her. She wouldn't have believed it possible, but she wanted him again. She'd thought her body was too tired, too sated, to want more. She'd been wrong. But hard on the heels of the desire that threatened to swamp her consciousness was the reminder that, all pleasure aside, she was supposed to be exploring *him*. Josh Tremont, the man.

"Yes," she replied again, this time more firmly. "I would."

"Excellent. You won't regret it."

But as the limousine pulled up outside her home and Josh walked her to her front door, Callie experienced a deep sense of foreboding that she most definitely would.

Eight

The next two days dragged on interminably, as Josh closeted himself in his office with intercultural advisors and the heads of his legal department. Even though only metres separated them by day, Callie felt as if they were suddenly worlds apart. If it hadn't been for the brief moments when their eyes met or their hands brushed as she handed him a file, she would have begun to wonder if she hadn't imagined their idyllic night together on the water.

Every time she looked out the wide expanse of his office window toward the harbour, she was reminded of what they'd shared and it made her want more. So very much more. And that was very dangerous indeed, because despite how hard she was falling for him, she had to remember her promise to Irene. She had to remember that Josh threatened the Palmers with every business move he made and somehow she had to find out why, and how to stop him.

She'd let Irene know that she would be spending the weekend with Josh and her mentor had expressed her approval.

"Make sure you find out whatever you can," she'd insisted. "Leave no stone unturned."

Finally, it was five o'clock on Friday afternoon and Callie was finalising her backup process when the hairs on the back of her neck prickled and a deep sense of awareness permeated her body.

"I thought this week would never end."

Josh's lips were close to her ear and she shivered as he bent his head to kiss her softly against the pulse that now fluttered erratically in her neck. He swivelled her chair around and drew her to her feet, pulling her against him and slanting his lips across hers like a man who'd been denied human contact for far too long.

Callie gave herself over to his embrace. She knew all too well how he felt.

"Let's go," he murmured against her lips. "Or I might not make it home."

Every muscle in her body clenched on the surge of arousal that swept through her. If he asked, she'd let him have her on her desk, the floor, anywhere as long as he'd assuage the clamouring need inside. It was probably just as well that he'd kept his distance these past two days or she'd have been a quivering wreck and rendered incapable of doing her job.

"My things are in the back of my car," she replied.

They travelled together in the elevator to the underground car park, stopping only for a few minutes for her to retrieve her bag before they were in the Maserati and driving along Tamaki Drive toward St Heliers.

Traffic along the waterfront was heavy and by the time Josh hit the automatic gate and garage door openers he was in a fever pitch to get Callie upstairs and into the master suite. If it hadn't been for the matter of protection, he would have eschewed the master suite in favour of any flat surface. He made a mental note to ensure that didn't become a problem in the near future.

He grabbed up her bag and took her hand and, after disarming the internal alarm system, led her up the main staircase and straight to his bedroom.

He almost hated the insatiable hunger that infused him when she was around. Hated it yet welcomed it with every breath in his body. Their physical union was an unexpected, yet very welcome, addition to their working relationship and Josh had no doubt it would take some considerable time to burn out.

Callie reached for him the second he slammed the bedroom door behind them—shoving his jacket off his shoulders and wrenching his shirttails from the waistband of his trousers. He loosened his tie and ripped it from beneath his collar even as she undid the buttons that ran down the front of his shirt. Then her hands were on his chest. He let out a groan as she scratched her nails lightly across the flat disks of his nipples.

She quickly replaced her nails with her lips, her teeth gently rasping over his tender skin while her hands slid down his abdomen and to his waistband. He felt his trousers slip down his legs, felt her hand reach deftly inside his briefs and then, gloriously, felt her free his erection—her fingers wrapping instinctively around him with just the right pressure.

Josh reached beneath her dress. Rucking the fabric up over her thighs, her hips, until he could tug at the scrap of nonsense she called underwear. His fingers slipped between her legs and he groaned again as he felt her wetness. He rubbed her sensitive flesh and caught her answering plea with his lips as she pressed herself harder against his fingers.

He walked her backwards until he felt her knees buckle against the side of the king-sized sleigh bed that dominated his room. She fell gently backwards onto the bed and Josh reached for the top drawer of his bedside cabinet, grabbing the box of condoms and scattering its contents onto the bed bedside them.

Callie's throaty laugh as she saw what he was doing caused him to smile in response, but then he was all seriousness as, sheathed, he positioned himself at her entrance. Dammit, but he'd planned to take it slow with her this weekend. Make every second, every stroke, count. But the fever that raged through his veins demanded to be assuaged right here, right now.

He plunged inside her welcoming heat and felt her inner muscles contract around him in a velvet fist. He nearly lost it right there, but somehow he found the strength to withdraw and drive home again, and again, until her scream of completion rent the air between them and he could finally let go with everything he had.

Wave after wave swamped him and he collapsed against Callie, his chest heaving, his heart thumping as if he'd completed a marathon. She sucked everything out of him in a way no woman had ever done before. When he was capable, he rolled onto his side and lay there next to her on the bed. Eventually, he propped himself up on an elbow.

"Are you okay?" he asked, smoothing a lock of hair from her face as she lay staring up at the ceiling, her legs still splayed, her dress still around her waist.

"I don't think I've ever been more okay in my life," she answered, turning her head to look at him. "How can it keep getting better?"

Josh smiled, a swell of pride rolling through him. "We have this weekend to find out. C'mon, we'll grab a quick shower then let's see about dinner."

He sat up and removed his shoes and socks, grinning ruefully at his total disarray as the incongruity of their appearance struck home. He kicked away his trousers and shrugged off his shirt before reaching for Callie and helping her to remove her dress and bra. He led her through to the cream-and-gold marble master bathroom and turned on the faucets in the massive double shower.

Slowly and tenderly he bathed her, taking extra care between her legs, trailing his soapy hands over her breasts and relishing their fullness before he rinsed her and pushed her gently from the shower stall.

"If you don't go now I won't be responsible for my actions," he explained.

Through the steamy enclosure he watched as she leisurely dried herself and walked naked back into the bedroom. Josh turned the faucets to full cold, standing beneath the needle-sharp spray until he knew he'd be able to follow her without throwing her back on the bed for round two.

Restraint, control. They'd been his touchstones for as long as he could remember, yet Callie Rose Lee had effectively rendered him useless in that regard. Somehow that didn't bother him as much as it should. He'd always sworn he'd never settle down until he'd avenged his mother's sorrow and made his father pay for his abandonment, but with Callie he almost began to wonder if his plan didn't need some revision. Whether there wasn't room for both in his life. It was certainly something worth exploring, he decided.

Saturday morning the weather turned to rain and as Josh had excused himself after breakfast to attend to an urgent call from one of his business contacts in Europe, Callie found herself with time on her hands and very little to do.

She wandered through the downstairs living room that led out to the pool area where they'd dined together only a week ago. She shook her head slightly. A week. It felt like so much longer.

Her body appeared to be in total agreement. Already she missed Josh's proximity with a physical ache—or maybe that ache had more to do with the way her body had been thoroughly, deliciously, used through the dark hours. A smile pulled at her lips.

She'd loved every second of last night. After they'd both dressed, they'd gone to the kitchen where they'd cooked a meal together, taking their plates out onto the tiled terrace where they sat on the descending stairs overlooking the pool. With their dinner balanced on their laps and a glass of red wine each, they'd eaten in companionable silence before heading back indoors.

They'd started to watch a movie in Josh's home theatre but it hadn't taken long before the gentle stroke of his fingers across the back of her hand had ignited desire once more. They hadn't even made it out of the room before their clothing had hit the carpet. Callie had to admit to a distinct soft spot for the wide and comfortable armchairs that had allowed for some inventive foreplay before Josh had pulled her to the floor where she'd straddled his body, taking him deep inside, and riding him to an incendiary climax.

Even now, the memory pulled at something deep inside her. Something she'd never allowed herself to feel before. Something that felt scarily like the beginnings of love.

Don't be crazy, she told herself sternly. You're not supposed to fall for the guy. You're supposed to be gathering information—and what had she discovered? Nothing other than the fact that he worked hard and expected the same in return from his people. That and the fact that the man made love like a dream. His hands, his mouth, he used everything in his arsenal to bring her pleasure such as she'd never known—and it was addictive. *He* was addictive.

Men like Josh Tremont should definitely come with a warning firmly plastered on their foreheads, she decided.

But still there was that niggle. Despite the man she was growing to know, there was still the matter of the information he'd gathered on the Palmers. He'd delved deeply into their personal lives. Knew every minor detail, right down to Bruce Palmer's dental appointments. It was bizarre and not a little obsessive.

Callie shook her head. Thinking about it wasn't going to prove anything. If she was to do what Irene expected of her, she needed to find out more details about Josh Tremont himself. More than the fact he was a completely unselfish lover. More than the fact that the mere sound of his footfall coming toward her on the polished wooden floor was enough to set her heart beating like the wings of a startled flock of pigeons.

"Sorry about that," he said as he moved behind her and slid his arms around her waist, pulling her back against him.

Callie inhaled deeply as his unique scent enveloped her. In itself it was an aphrodisiac to her. Already her body stirred in response. She laughed inwardly. At this rate she'd barely be able to move by Monday.

"I imagine you're never fully off duty," Callie replied, relishing the feeling of protection she felt within the circle of his arms.

"I promise you have my undivided attention for the rest of this weekend. What would you like to do today?"

A squall of rain splattered against the glass doors in front of them.

"I suppose a swim is out of the question," Callie said, gesturing to the rain-washed terrace and sheets of rain that peppered the tiles.

"Why should it be? It's been years since I swam in the rain. How about you?"

Callie gave an inelegant snort. "I don't think I've ever swum in the rain."

"Not even as a kid?"

"Especially not as a kid."

In fact, she hadn't learned to swim until she'd been at the Palmer Home for Girls. At first the prospect of putting her face under water had terrified her, but eventually she'd overcome that fear and had learned to use the experience to tackle bigger fears, bigger problems, and overcome them. It was another opportunity Irene had opened up to her. Another reason to be grateful.

"So how about it?"

Callie thought it over for a minute. She'd had little enough time in her life for frivolous fun, now here she was at twenty-eight and she hadn't even done something as fun and simple as swim in the rain.

"Yes," she nodded her head. "I'd love to. But I didn't bring my swimsuit."

"Who said we need to wear a swimsuit?"

A spear of something electric jolted through her. Swim in the nude?

"What about your neighbours? Can't they see the pool?"

Josh gestured outside. "There's no one who overlooks us here. It's one of the things that drew me to this place. We have complete privacy."

Josh led her through a covered walkway from the side of the house to the poolhouse set off to one side. There, they undressed and ventured out into the rain.

Callie squealed as the cool raindrops hit her, sending her into a half jog toward the pool. At her side, Josh dived cleanly into the water, surfacing about halfway along and encouraging her to join him.

She took a deep breath and dived in. Not as clean as Josh's entry to the water but competent enough, she decided as she cut through the water. The deliciously erotic sensation against her body was like gliding through silk. The pool was warmer than the rain and the contrast against her skin when she surfaced was invigorating. Laughter bubbled from deep inside.

How long had it been since she'd indulged in something purely for fun. Aside from her shoe habit, which she acknowledged had deeper-seated issues, she tended not to let her hair down like this. And it was way past time she did.

"What do you think?" Josh asked as he swam toward her.

"Bliss," she smiled in return.

Callie floated onto her back, her eyes closed, relishing the sensation of the rain dancing on the surface of her skin. Josh stood beside her and supported her with his arms before lowering his head to lick raindrops off her breasts. Callie felt the feather-light touch all the way to her core and she moaned with pleasure as he suckled gently at her nipples.

"Now we're talking bliss," he murmured.

He seemed to magically know exactly where and how to touch her. Exactly what would make her slow burn and what would strike an inferno. She delighted in the gentle teasing he did now, allowing him to support her weight in the water.

When he suggested that they leave the pool, she was more than ready, and when he dried her slowly in the cabana, before lowering her to the daybed, she thought she couldn't feel more alive or happier than she felt at that moment.

Later, after they'd dressed and made their way back to the main house, they worked together in the kitchen to prepare lunch. They ate in the informal lounge off the kitchen, joking with one another about water sports.

"You don't have fun often, do you?"

His question was blunt and came out of left field, catching Callie by surprise.

"Of course I have fun."

"Then why have you never skinny-dipped before, or even swum in the rain."

"Not everyone gets the opportunity, you know."

"In New Zealand? It doesn't take money to be able

to do those things. Most of us live within shouting distance of some body of water."

"My parents were never into swimming."

No, she remembered, they indulged in other, darker, things. Things that didn't include their only daughter and for which she was always in the way.

"Callie, what were they into?"

"Stuff. None of it good. Let's just say they weren't involved in the usual family pursuits and leave it at that."

Josh lifted a hand and gently stroked one finger over her cheek. "I'm sorry about that."

Callie shrugged. "I survived."

"Yeah, but every child deserves more than survival."

There was a thread of bitterness to his voice that surprised her. That same hint of anger she'd observed in him last weekend when he'd talked about his mother.

"You didn't exactly have it easy yourself, did you." She made it more of a statement than a question.

"No, I didn't."

Josh tugged Callie across the two-seater they shared, and into his lap. She snuggled against him, loving the way her body curved to fit his.

"Tell me about it," she coaxed.

As much as she felt like she was intruding on what was obviously intensely private, she hoped he could give her a clue as to why he was so intent on knowing everything there was to know about the Palmers, and why he seemed determined to destabilise their business. As much as it sickened her to have to pry, she knew that if she could get the information that Irene wanted, then, and only then, could she hope to allow her relationship with Josh to become something real. And it shocked her to admit just how real she wanted it to be.

Today had made her realise that she'd had enough of being someone else's pawn, and she was sick of false pretences. Instead of allowing herself to simply enjoy being with Josh and letting her feelings for him take their natural course, she had to second-guess herself all the way. It was time the deceitfulness ended. But even as she reached her decision, she knew she could do nothing until she'd delivered on her promise to Irene. There was something about Josh that probably wasn't the truth, either, and she had to find that something out.

"Long story short? My mother worked for an older married man. She had an affair with him. She got pregnant with me. He tried to buy her off with $10,000 and made her move away."

Callie couldn't hold back the cry of sympathy that rose from her heart. She knew all about rejection. She'd experienced it nearly every day of the first sixteen years of her life.

"So, yeah, I have some idea of what it's like to survive. If he'd shown once ounce of respect for her and her feelings, things wouldn't have been as bad for her as they were."

"Surely he owed her more than that. Couldn't she have applied through the courts for support for you?"

"Her pride would never let her. I think she was so

hurt when he rejected her that she decided to just disappear off the radar. She changed her surname from Morrisey and adopted her mother's maiden name and then set out to give me the best childhood she could."

"So you still got to swim in the rain and go skinny-dipping?" Callie asked with a gentle smile.

"I did—and more. There wasn't a day that went by that I didn't know she loved me more than life itself. That's the kind of gift you take for granted until it's gone."

"At least you had that."

"Yeah, I did. And I promised her that one day I'd make it up to her, but she died before I could give her what she deserved."

"And your father? He still didn't help you, even when she died?"

Josh's bark of laughter lacked humour in any form. "No, I came across his contact details in her things when she died. Up until then I didn't even know who he was. Mum would never talk about him and whenever I'd bring it up she'd change the subject. Then, later, I'd always hear her crying in her room. It doesn't take too many times before a kid realises his need to know takes a back seat to his mother's happiness."

Josh shifted to one side, letting Callie slide from his lap. He rose and walked over to the bookcase that lined one wall of the room. On one shelf stood a small box, like a miniature pirate's chest. He lifted it with both hands and turned back to Callie.

"She always kept this at her bedside. Locked, of course, although that didn't stop me trying to get into it," he admitted with a rueful smile. "She was good at hiding things, though, and I only found the key after she'd died."

He dug into his trouser pocket and pulled out his keys and, selecting the smallest, opened the box. From where she sat Callie could see the yellow paper of a stack of envelopes, tied together with a length of faded pink silk ribbon.

"They're letters, from him. He stopped writing when she got pregnant with me."

"Have you read them?" Callie asked, feeling as if she was poised at the edge of a precipice. Were these letters the key to what Irene needed?

"Yeah, I made myself read every one of them—even the letter and cheque that were sent to my mother, paying her off and telling her to get out of town."

"She never cashed the cheque? Why? She must have desperately needed the money."

"As I said before, her pride wouldn't let her. I think she felt she'd lost so much already that she wasn't prepared to lose that, too."

"I can't believe you've kept them all this time. Wouldn't it be better to destroy them, to let go?"

"They were my only contact with a father I'd never known. I've kept his lies as a reminder of what he owed my mother—what he owed me. And I vowed on my mother's grave that I'd make him pay one day."

"Josh, surely you can't mean that," Callie protested. "Everyone has to learn to let go eventually."

She levered herself up and out of the seat and crossed

the room to take the box from his hands and place it back on the bookcase next to him. She slid her arms around his waist, desperate to offer him comfort, but he remained rigid in her embrace.

"Oh, yes," he replied, his voice hard and strangely detached, a total contrast to the warm, loving companion she'd known over the weekend. "I mean every word of it. He'll regret that he didn't do what was right. He'll regret every word of his lies and the world will finally know what a two-faced bastard he really is. And when he's forced to publicly acknowledge me, he will know that he, and he alone, was the master of his own destruction."

A finger of dread touched Callie's heart. She had no doubt that Josh would follow through on his promise, and she would hate to be in the shoes of the man he targeted. If there was anything she was certain of at this moment, it was that Josh was a man driven by his emotions—and given those emotions, what would he do to her when he found out the truth about why she was here?

Nine

That night when they made love there was an edge of desperation to Josh's touch—a driven hunger that Callie ached to assuage—but she knew, even as she finally drifted to sleep in his arms, that she could never remedy what ailed his heart.

The next morning, after a night of fractured sleep, she slipped from the bed and went downstairs. If she couldn't sleep, at least she could make herself useful and put together something for them to enjoy for breakfast.

It was as she passed through to the kitchen her eyes were drawn to the small chest sitting on the bookcase. Still open. She hesitated a moment, then, with a tentative hand, slid the top envelope out from under the ribbon.

The postmark was dated more than thirty years ago and the masculine handwriting on the envelope stood out in stark black lines. Callie slid open the flap and unfolded the sheets of paper within. No matter how stark the bold strokes of the handwriting they could not detract from the words of love that filled the page. Callie felt a lump form in her throat as she read the first page filled with private words of love between a man and his mistress. Words that spoke of his frustration in being trapped in a marriage of propriety and expectation. A marriage that was barren of the joy of children.

These weren't the words of a man who lied, of that Callie was certain. She felt as if she were intruding to read any more, as if she were trespassing on what had been a deeply intimate connection between two people. She refolded the sheets and slid the letter back into its envelope. The sheer depth of emotion she'd felt reading that single page filled her with a sense of helplessness and, yes, even envy that one woman had been the object of a man's love and devotion to such an extent. Her fingers trembled as she replaced the envelope in the stack and carefully closed the lid on the chest Callie firmly believed should have been buried with its owner. The letters didn't deserve to be used as a tool for revenge.

They were private, a glimpse into the love and loss between two people who loved at the wrong time. A couple destined to be torn apart.

She couldn't help wondering whether it would be the

same for her and Josh. He wouldn't suffer her betrayal in silence. He'd come for her with all guns blazing, unless she could somehow satisfy Irene's demands without him finding out.

Somehow, she didn't fancy her chances.

Irene had celebrated a birthday over the weekend, and Callie had promised to stop in and see her at home after work on Monday. As she drove over the Harbour Bridge to their Northcote Point address, she couldn't help but keep an eye on her rearview mirror. Her double life was beginning to mess with her mind, and she castigated herself as a paranoic fool for believing that Josh even suspected her of any duplicity. He wasn't the kind of man to put a tail on her. Oh, no. If he had any idea of what she was up to, he'd confront her, up front and personal, and demand his answers in no uncertain terms.

Callie's heart ached with the fear of him finding out. The more time she spent with him, the more she could feel herself falling in love with him, piece by inexorable piece. And she knew that was a recipe for disaster. To even begin to think that her love might be returned was destined for failure. She was in an untenable position unless she told Irene she could no longer fulfil her promise.

The very thought filled her with trepidation. She owed Irene everything and she'd felt honour-bound to repay the older woman with her loyalty. All of which made what she was about to do very, very difficult. She couldn't go through with it. Not any longer. Irene's obsession with Josh Tremont was unfounded. The two corporations worked on the same playing field, competed for the same work, time and time again. Yes, Josh had had a mole in the Palmer Enterprises structure, which weakened their chances, but now that that mole had been exposed, surely Irene could let go of her fears and rely on the Palmers' business acumen and longstanding reputation to hold their own.

And let Callie fall in love with Josh.

Callie gripped the steering wheel tight as she took the turnoff that led to the cliff-top home of the Palmer family. She wondered how they'd feel, leaving it all behind to take up the consular position in Guildara.

She punched in the security code at the gate and coasted down the driveway, all the while fighting back the nerves that threatened to send her stomach into orbit.

Irene was her usual impeccable self, rising from the sofa in the formal lounge as Callie was shown in.

"How are you, my dear?" she asked, bussing Callie on the cheek as she greeted her. "You look tired. I hope that man isn't demanding too much of you."

No more than she willingly gave him, Callie thought to herself as she forced a smile and shook her head.

Irene exclaimed over Callie's gift to her, a vintage Chanel handbag they'd seen on a shopping expedition together months earlier. It had cost far more than Callie would ordinarily spend on a gift, but Irene was worth it. Without her steady hand guiding Callie's life, who knew where she'd have ended up?

"Callie, it's beautiful. How clever of you to remember how much I liked this. Here," she said, handing Callie the birthday card she'd included with the gift, "pop this up on the mantel with the others."

Callie took the card and crossed the room to the wide white marble fireplace. She put her card among the colourful collection already there and idly picked up the card next to it to read the message inside.

It was from Bruce Palmer to Irene. The usual generic kind of card a husband bought for his wife, but personalised with his own message inside. In his own handwriting. Handwriting that was suddenly far too familiar. Handwriting Callie had seen only yesterday in passionate declarations of love to another woman.

Her heart shuddered to a halt in her chest, kick-starting again with an erratic beat that made her fingers suddenly nerveless and saw the card flutter from her hands to the floor.

She bent to pick the card up again, and studied the lettering once more. There was no mistake. His distinctive slanting hand leapt from the card, damning him with every stroke. Ignoring her instinct to rent the card in two, Callie carefully placed it back on the mantel, barely able to draw breath.

"Are you all right, dear? You're very pale."

Irene's voice swam through the fog in Callie's mind. Callie had to get out of there. She couldn't stay and go through the motions of a late-afternoon tea with the woman who'd been deceived by her husband for more than thirty-five years.

It was all too much. Somehow she had to gather her thoughts together and she knew she couldn't do that with Irene sitting directly opposite her. Not today. Not when the realisation was all too raw and monumental in her mind.

"Actually, if you don't mind I won't stay, Irene. I'm sorry, but I'm really not feeling all that well. Can I call you a bit later in the week?"

"Certainly, but will you be all right to drive home?"

"Yes, I'll be fine. I think I need an early night is all. Again, I'm very sorry."

"Don't even think about it," Irene said. "We'll catch up before the weekend and you can get me up-to-date on Tremont at the same time."

How she made it out to her car and safely home was a mystery to her, but the instant Callie set foot inside her house she crumbled. On legs that had the consistency of overcooked spaghetti she made it up the stairs to her bedroom where she threw herself onto her covers and lay, eyes burning, staring at the ceiling.

The truth stared her starkly in the face. Bruce Palmer had to be the married man Josh's mum had had the affair with.

Bruce was Josh's father.

Callie couldn't reconcile the head of Palmer Enterprises with the man whose intimate thoughts she'd read in a letter to his mistress. Nor could she reconcile that man, the lover, with the one who'd rejected both his mistress and his unborn child so callously.

Josh Tremont and Adam Palmer were about the same

age. Irene had obviously gotten pregnant around the same time as Josh's mother, and with the benefit of a legitimate heir in his near future, Bruce had clearly chosen to shun the woman he'd professed to love.

Or had it all been a lie, as Josh had said? Had he never loved Josh's mother? Had he just seen a pretty face in the workplace and, using the power and charisma of his position, wooed her into his bed?

It just didn't seem right. Bruce Palmer had always had such a dignity about him. She knew about the loss of one of his twin sons shortly after birth and had been told that afterwards he'd poured himself heart and soul into his work, almost at the expense of everything and everyone else.

Were those the actions of a man who'd discarded his illegitimate child without another thought? It just didn't feel right. And yet, it had happened. Josh had the proof. He had the curt letter of dismissal, the cheque his mother had never cashed, all there in the bundle of letters.

Callie's heart ached for Josh and for his dead mother. They'd had nothing and no one but each other, and they could have had so much more. Bruce Palmer could have ensured their financial security with very little hardship to himself. It would have been the right thing to do. The honourable thing to do.

Suddenly, Callie was faced with the awful truth that a man she'd long admired was not who she'd thought he was. Above all else, what could she now tell Irene? The woman expected answers, truthful answers.

Bile rose in Callie's throat, forcing her upright and into her bathroom. She clung to the cold surface of her bathroom vanity as thoughts tumbled through her head, one after the other.

Now she understood Josh's relentless pursuit of Palmer Enterprises and his apparent aim of bringing the company down around Bruce's ears. Fear made her stomach lurch and Callie fought to keep it under control.

What did Josh plan to do, she wondered? At what stage would he play out the final stages of a drama she had no doubt he'd planned for years. He'd said he would force his father to publicly acknowledge him. He obviously planned to use the letters to do so.

Realisation dawned. She knew exactly when Josh planned to go public. At the time it would do the most damage to Bruce's credibility. The consul announcement would be made on Christmas Eve and she knew there'd be much feting and fanfare surrounding it. The truth about Bruce's behaviour—about the woman he'd used and discarded and the son he'd ignored—would be blown into the stratosphere of tabloid gossip.

The Palmers stood to lose everything they held dear.

Callie ran cold water in the basin and splashed it against her face. What should she do now? Did she go to Irene and tell her the truth? Shatter the very foundation of what she'd built her life around? Tears filled Callie's eyes and began to tumble in a steady stream down her cheeks as she realised she could never be the one to destroy Irene's world. Not when Irene had been the one to create one for Callie.

So where did that leave her? Did she warn Bruce that his bastard son was hell-bent on revenge? Or could she forestall Josh, confront him about his father? Beg him to withdraw from the retribution that was honestly his? By her reckoning she had four weeks before the announcement was due to be made. That was four weeks in which she had to turn things around. Right now she had no idea what to do.

"What do you mean Palmers beat us to the punch on this one? We had this deal all but signed."

Josh glared at the assembled management team in the boardroom and scoured their faces for any hint of what had gone wrong.

"Josh, we don't understand it ourselves. Somehow they must have gotten an inside track on our proposal," one of the executives offered.

An inside track? Josh pondered the ramifications of that suggestion for a split second before speaking again.

"Is there any way we can block them? Go lower? Offer more?"

"It's a done deal. The trade ministry has signed off on it already."

Josh swore, long and low, before dismissing his team.

"This had better not happen again," he growled to his legal advisor as the man held back after everyone else had filed out of the room.

"Josh, there's no way the leak came from any of them. They hadn't even been made privy to your final proposal before Palmers swooped in under us."

"What are you suggesting?"

"That maybe you've been employing the same under-handed tactics yourself for so long that now you can't even trust your own men. Think about it, Josh. Who else could have disseminated that information? Who else might have something to gain by it? Either your computer system was breached externally by some hacker, or perhaps you need to look a little closer to your own office before you start accusing these guys of foul play."

His own office? There were only two people who had access to his computer. Himself and once, very briefly, Callie—and he knew for damn certain *he* hadn't shared his proposal with Palmers.

Had she double-crossed him? An ember of fury flared to life deep in his gut. The evidence certainly pointed to it. Had she hoodwinked him all along? A wave of disgust nearly swamped him. He'd allowed his libido to rule his head. He'd let her get close. He'd seen her, wanted her, had her and he'd shared truths with her he'd never shared with any other person.

Above all, he'd trusted her. The words she'd uttered weeks ago now came back to haunt him, *"Seems you ought to be more concerned about the loyalty of people you can buy."*

People like her, maybe?

If it was true that she'd betrayed him, she would pay for her deceit, along with that of her old boss. He'd make sure they were both hung out to dry. It shouldn't be too hard to find out where her loyalties lay.

Palmers would be high on the success of this latest

contract, they'd be eager to do the same again—to pip him at the post—and this time he would let them. An idea began to formulate in his mind. He'd have to be careful, but he knew he could do it, and prove Callie's innocence or guilt at the same time.

And when he carried this one off, he'd have destroyed his competition for good.

Ten

It was two days since she'd made her discovery and she still had no idea of what she was going to do. In the office, Josh had been the same as ever—focussed, professional—yet every now and then she'd caught him watching her as if something else weighed on his mind. They hadn't been intimate since the weekend, and she found herself missing that special closeness they'd shared.

She started at her desk, her senses on instant alert as Josh came through from his office.

"Callie, I'd like you to type up these notes now—top priority and top level confidentiality. Make certain you password the file with this code."

She noted the code he'd written on the top of the sheets of his hand-scrawled notes.

"Do you want these back when I've completed the computer file or should I destroy them?"

"Destroy them. The file is all we'll need."

He turned to go back into his office.

"Josh? Is everything okay?" she asked, rising from her seat and walking over to him.

To her relief, he smiled and bent down slightly to kiss her cheek.

"Everything's fine, just busy—making up for losing the Flinders contract to Palmers."

Callie felt guilt run cold through her veins. The Flinders contract had been the one she'd given the information on to Irene. It was what she'd had to do at the time, but now she wished she'd never agreed to be the go-between in this crazy game. She wasn't cut out for the subterfuge or the emotional cost it demanded.

"With any luck, the material you're working on today will cover that quite nicely," Josh smiled. "Are you busy tonight?"

Callie dragged her thoughts together. "No, I don't have any plans."

"Let's have dinner together."

"I tell you what," she started, thinking quickly. She didn't want the anonymity of some restaurant tonight. She needed Josh's attention on her and only her if she was to assure herself that nothing was wrong between them. "Why don't I cook for you?"

"Are you sure you wouldn't rather go out?"

"I'm certain," she said, nodding for good measure. "What time will you be finished tonight?"

"I've got that meeting away from the office at four-thirty," he considered, and she could see him mentally juggling how long it would be expected to take. "I can be at your place by seven, but why don't you go around to my place instead. It's closer to where I'll be and I can get there to be with you sooner."

"Perfect. I'll bring everything over for dinner."

"Bring a change of clothes for tomorrow while you're at it," he said. He handed her an electronic key. "Here, you'll need this. It'll open the gate and garage door. Just leave the gate open for me."

"And the alarm?"

He repeated a numerical code, which she committed to memory.

Excitement unfurled within her. Clearly, he couldn't suspect her of wrongdoing. She still stood a chance of making things work, of maybe even turning his need for revenge into something else. Realistically, she knew she'd be fighting against a current that had roared through his life for far too long, but she had to hope that somehow she could make a difference.

The sheaf of notes Josh had given Callie were extensive. How he'd managed to corner another proposal so quickly after losing the Flinders job explained why he was so successful. As Callie automatically transcribed his crabbed handwriting, she started to mentally plan for the evening ahead. She wanted everything to be perfect.

It was exactly a month until Christmas. Would it be too early to give him a gift? Perhaps herself, gift-wrapped in something special? At lunchtime she found the perfect thing. A rich burgundy satin nightgown and matching organza peignoir. She couldn't wait to see Josh's face when she wore it.

It was nearly five o'clock before she finished typing up the notes. She was getting her handbag from her drawer, in readiness to leave the office, when the strident shriek of the building alarm cut through her thoughts like a hot knife through butter. She knew the routine—drill or genuine alarm, she had to leave her office immediately.

As far as confidentiality was concerned, everything on her computer was set to auto backup already, and her computer itself would lock down without activity within five minutes. But that left the notes Josh had given her. She hadn't shredded them yet and had no time to do that now.

Callie folded the sheets up and shoved them in her bag. She'd have to shred them when she came back once the building had the all-clear, but she couldn't leave them lying around. As she joined the throng of staff members in the stairwell, and steeled herself for the long climb to the ground floor, she hoped this was only a drill and that they'd be back inside soon.

Her hopes were dashed as she waited at the staff assembly point. A small fire had started elsewhere in the building and the fire department had said it would be some time before they'd be letting everyone back in.

The news was met with groans of dismay as most people would have to wait for the all-clear to be able to go inside and recover their means to return home.

Callie thanked her lucky stars she had her bag with her. While she couldn't get into the underground car park to retrieve her car until the building was reopened, she could certainly taxi home and then taxi to Josh's place. Once cleared by the building warden that she could go, she did exactly that.

The cab driver was all too happy to stop outside a nearby supermarket so she could gather the ingredients she wanted for the dinner she'd planned tonight, and then, for a nominal extra fee, to wait while she rushed inside her town house and gathered her things for the night ahead.

By the time she reached Josh's house, she was racing. She dropped the ingredients for her dinner preparations in the kitchen. She put on a large pot of water to boil, and set to work slicing onions and garlic together with mushrooms and bacon for the fettuccine she'd decided on. At least the meal was quick and easy to prepare.

She hummed to herself as the aromas from the fry pan blended together and she added the ribbons of fresh pasta to the boiling water before stirring in cream and parmesan to the ingredients in the pan. The fresh pasta was ready in minutes and, once drained and lightly tossed with the sauce, she slid the whole mixture into a large shallow bowl, covered it with foil and set it in the oven to keep warm.

A quick cleanup in the kitchen and she was ready to race upstairs to the master bedroom where she stripped off her work clothes and underwear and slid into the nightgown and peignoir. She took a minute to freshen her fragrance, the spritz between her breasts sending a shimmer of something more to spiral through her.

The swish of her nightgown between her thighs as she made her way back downstairs started up a thrill of longing that beat from her core. She couldn't wait for Josh to arrive home. A smile danced across her lips. There was something deliciously decadent about not wearing any undergarments. It ranked right up there with skinny-dipping in the rain.

Callie distracted herself by setting the dining room table and searched out a couple of candles to dress it up a little. She remembered seeing some lovely squat scented candles in the living room the last time she was here.

In the living room her eyes were inexorably drawn to the bookcase and, more particularly, to the small chest that sat there. In it lay the seed of Josh's bitterness. The only physical evidence he had to say who his father really was.

Callie reached out and let her fingers rest on the lid. What would Josh be like now, she wondered, if those letters had never existed? Would he have been as driven to triumph in his chosen market? Had his very need for revenge been the catalyst that saw him reach the heights he knew today or would he have gotten there anyway? Had his father, by his neglect, inversely created Josh's success?

In the distance she heard a door slam and she jumped, knocking the box. Surprisingly, the lid jumped, too. Josh hadn't relocked it. She lifted the lid cautiously, as if doing so would unleash the miseries of Pandora's box, then let the lid drop closed again. Obviously, he'd forgotten.

Footsteps echoed on the parquet floor of the entrance hall as Josh came through from the garage. She snatched her hand away and wheeled from the bookcase, all thoughts of the box and its contents banished from her mind as he entered the room.

"Something smells good," he commented. "I was worried you might be late. I got a call about the tower."

"Nothing was going to stop me being here with you tonight," Callie said as she eased into his embrace and lifted her face for his kiss.

Her heart beat double-time in her chest by the time he released her.

"Dinner's ready," she said, slipping from his arms. "I was just getting some candles for the table."

"It can wait," Josh growled, reaching for her again. "Right now I want you."

"Right now?"

Excitement thrilled through her.

"Oh, yes."

Josh swept her up into his arms and headed straight up the stairs, his breath barely showing signs of any strain. In his bedroom he kicked the door closed behind them and gently lowered her to her feet.

"I like this," he said, pushing aside her peignoir and sweeping his hand over the slinky fabric of her nightgown.

"It feels beautiful, but—" his hand slid under the hem of the gown and pushed upward until he cupped her bottom "—I like the feel of you more."

"It's your early Christmas gift," Callie gasped.

Rational thought fled her mind as his fingers slid over her buttocks and then traced down until they reached the cleft between her thighs. Heat and moisture gathered there as his fingers teased her sensitive flesh.

"So that means I get to unwrap it," he said with a smile.

Josh withdrew his hand, quickly slipped out of his jacket and yanked his tie out from under the collar of his shirt. Several buttons popped as he undid his shirt and pulled it free from his trousers. Callie could only stand and watch as he stripped down to his black briefs, and tremble as he walked toward her—his eyes darkest blue, his face a mask of determined perfection.

He reached for her and eased the peignoir from her shoulders, stopping to kiss each exposed inch of flesh until she quivered with desire. He eased her back onto the bed and trailed his fingers from her ankles upward to the hem of the gown, then, with his hands clenched in the satin, he pushed the fabric up, exposing her to him.

His eyes darkened even more as he gazed upon her. If it were possible, she felt even wetter, more primed for him than she was already. And when he bent his head to her, taking her in his mouth, swirling her flesh with his tongue, grazing her nerve endings ever so softly with his teeth, she let her eyes close, her head drop back, and gave herself over to sensation.

It was dark by the time they finally made their way back downstairs to eat dinner. Even though the meal had dried out somewhat in the oven, that did nothing to deter their appetite. Eventually, they took their glasses and the opened bottle of wine upstairs to attend to other, undiminished hungers.

Afterwards, Josh fell into a deep slumber. Despite the lateness and her own weariness, Callie couldn't sleep. Instead, she watched the man at her side, bathed in silver strands of moonlight, and never more beautiful to her than he'd ever been before. Her heart swelled with the solid truth that she finally allowed herself to admit. She loved him. Totally, and wholly.

She wished she could do something, anything, to release him from the demons that drove him. To allow him the surcease of acceptance. But that was something only he could attain. He had to want it, embrace it.

His plans for revenge against Bruce Palmer and his family were what propelled him, what gave his work purpose. But what of the man? Could he ever let go of the bitterness inside, even if he saw his plan through? And what of the damage to the Palmers?

Callie knew what Bruce had done all those years ago was unforgivable, but time had a way of blurring the edges. Even though his behaviour with Josh's mother had been reprehensible, his life afterwards had been anything but. Callie was certain he hadn't so much as put a foot wrong in all the years since. He'd built his family and his business and he'd given to the community and the country unstintingly; hence the accolade of the upcoming consular position.

Maybe his behaviour had been his own way of compensating for the way he'd treated Josh and his mother. Who knew? But Callie understood better than most that his appointment as the honorary consul to Guildara was based on Bruce Palmer, the man. The man he was now.

Was it fair to destroy that? She didn't think so. Bruce still had so much good to give to the world. If Josh had his way, the older man would be destroyed. Pilloried in the public eye. Despite what he'd done to Josh, Callie still owed it to Bruce not to let that happen.

She slid from the bed and reached for her peignoir, not even fully understanding what she was about to do, just knowing in her heart of hearts that she had to do it. She had to destroy the contents of that box before Josh could use them against Bruce. Hopefully, then Josh could begin to heal the scar on his own heart.

Moonlight shone bright into the sitting room, but even if it had been pitch dark Callie knew she'd unerringly be able to find her target. She took the box from its place on the bookshelf. Her heart beat a staccato rhythm as she lifted the lid and removed the stack of envelopes inside.

She knew she had no right to do this. No right at all. But someone had to stop the cycle of hurt. Someone had to put an end to the anger and the accusations.

She moved over to the deep fireplace set into the wall

and knelt on the hearth. She knew she'd seen a fire-lighter somewhere in the inglenook. Her fingers closed over the very item she was looking for and she breathed a silent prayer of thanks.

Callie set the firelighter on the hearth next to the bundle of letters and undid the ribbon that bound them together. A twinge of sorrow cut through her at the thought that the love contained within the words on those pages would be destroyed forever. But, she ratio-nalised, that very love had wrought the complete opposite effect. And that effect had to be stopped now.

She lifted one envelope from the top of the stack and held it over the grate, her fingers shaking as she clicked the small ignition switch on the firelighter over and over again. A faint blue spark appeared at the end of the firelighter. A blue spark that with a small hiss turned into a golden flame.

She could feel the tears now, feel them burn within her eyes and scald her cheeks as she put the flame to the paper. The edge of the envelope lit up, glowing briefly before darkness consumed it, blackening the paper even as its contents had blackened Josh's heart.

Callie was sobbing now, lifting the next envelope and the next, adding them to the tiny blaze.

Light unexpectedly flooded the room and Callie heard a male shout. Josh peremptorily pushed her aside, a small fire extinguisher in his hands. He dealt with the flames, snatching the lesser-damaged letters from the fireplace and spreading them on the hearth where they smouldered like the fury etched on his face.

Looking up into his eyes, Callie knew this was the end of all she'd hoped for. The end of all her dreams. He'd never forgive her for this. Never understand that she'd done it for him.

Eleven

"What the hell do you think you're doing?" Josh ground out through a jaw clenched so tight he thought his teeth would shatter.

Callie just looked at him in horror.

Rage soared through him like a live creature, consuming reason and making his vision blur angry and red. He wanted to grab her, shake the truth from her, but he knew if he caved in to that urge he'd be unaccountable for his actions.

As if she could read his mind, she scooted out of his reach and drew upright, fear painting her already pale features even more pallid.

"I had to do it, Josh."

"Had to? You have no right. Those are my private property. You know what they are to me."

Josh fought to control his temper when all he really wanted to do was throw her bodily from the house.

"I know Bruce Palmer is your father. I can't let you use those letters against him."

"You can't?" he repeated incredulously. "It has nothing to do with you. Absolutely nothing."

"But it does, don't you see? I have to protect them. They saved me from the most awful life, Josh. I had hit my lowest ebb. They *saved* me! You have no idea. I owe it to them to do everything in my power to stop you from destroying them and yourself in the process."

"You set out to ensnare me from the beginning, didn't you?" he accused, taking a step toward her, his hands clenched into fists at his side. "This, everything, it's all been one lie after another."

"No! I didn't even want to take your damn job. I loved my work with Irene," she protested.

"Then why? Why did you come to work with me?"

"You only wanted *me* to hurt *them*. What does it matter?"

"Why did you come to work with me?" He enunciated each word so carefully he thought his mind would burst with the concentration it took.

Callie dropped her head. When she spoke he was hard-pressed to hear her.

"Irene wanted me to spy on you."

"Spy? On me?" Josh let loose a laugh that echoed hollowly through the room. "So you were behind the

Flinders information leak. Well, isn't that just kismet. All along I thought you were mine and there you were, betraying me to the very scum that made my mother's life a living hell."

Callie flinched at the harshness of his words but he couldn't feel any sympathy for the emotional blow he'd struck her.

"Josh, this anger you bear toward him—it's eating you up inside. It's taking away everything decent, everything your mother raised you to be, and replacing it with something cruel and vindictive. Have you ever actually *read* those letters?" She flung a hand at the charred envelopes on the hearth.

"I read them once. That was enough."

"Then you really don't understand and you never will. I had to get rid of them before they consumed everything that I love in you."

"Love?" He felt as if something vile had crawled into his mouth as he said the word. "You're trying to tell me that you love me?"

"I do!" she cried, her hands now clenched together in front of her. "I tried not to. Lord knows, it was the last thing I expected or wanted. I couldn't have been with you the way we have if I didn't love you. Josh, you're the first man I've made *love* with."

"Don't lie to me. You were no shrinking virgin when I took you."

"No, I wasn't, but I'm telling you the truth. I made some choices about sex when I was young—choices that had nothing to do with emotion. On the streets a girl can get to the stage where she'll do almost anything for a meal and shelter in the middle of a freezing winter night, especially when she hasn't eaten in a week. I'm not proud of what I did, but the fact remains I did what I had to do to survive. But after that last time I swore to myself that I'd rather die than let anyone touch me like that again—unless I loved him and trusted him, like I love and trust you. Josh, I never knew sex could be anything more. I never knew lovemaking could be like it is with you."

There was a painful thread of truth in her voice that made Josh step back and take stock. She obviously believed she loved him, which left only one more thing.

"If that's true, then you now have to make a choice, don't you?"

"Choice?" Confusion rippled over her features.

"Stand by me or stick with the Palmers."

"I…"

Her hesitation told him all he needed to know. Josh snorted in disgust. "I thought so. You still choose them, don't you?"

Callie didn't speak.

"Get out," he said, his voice near feral with resentment. "Get out of my house, get out of my life. I don't want you. Get out now!"

He tried to find some satisfaction in how swiftly she left the room and flew up the stairs. In minutes she was back down, fully dressed and carrying her overnight bag and handbag.

"Josh," she implored from the doorway, "please

rethink this. Promise me you'll read the letters again. Really read them this time. Talk to me when you've calmed down, when you can see reason."

"Oh, I see reason just fine. You know, you might not be a Palmer by birth, but you're no different from them at all. You're still cut from the same rotten cloth."

The resounding echo of the front door slamming behind her told him he'd made his mark, and yet, in the lingering stench of burned promises all he could feel was an emptiness that cut to his spirit and left him bleeding inside.

Love. What did she know about love? If she loved him, she'd stand by him, not try to undermine what he'd planned since he was eighteen years old.

He knelt and picked up the remains of her destruction and thanked his lucky stars that he'd missed her presence in the bed and awakened. If he hadn't, she'd have destroyed everything.

A couple of the letters were charred beyond redemption but others had escaped the damage of the flames and the extinguisher. He returned those to the box and carefully replaced it on the bookcase. There was still enough damning evidence to do what he wanted, and he would do it. He'd see this thing through to its bitter end.

Callie entered her office in the Palmer Enterprises tower and fought back the emptiness that threatened to swamp her. She should be relieved that she still had a job to come back to. A job she'd secured by spying on

Josh and subsequently ensuring Palmers' financial viability in the marketplace.

Reluctance now dogged her every step. In the past, she couldn't wait to start each day at Irene's side. Everything had brought her a measure of satisfaction and a sense of knowing she'd completed a job well done. But it was as if she operated in shades of grey. There was no colour in her life, no joy.

From the time she'd called a taxi on her mobile phone, from the top of Josh's driveway, until the second she'd walked back into Irene's business suite she'd been encased in ice. It was only as she'd opened her handbag and seen that she still had Josh's notes inside that some sense of life had permeated the frozen shell around her. That life had brought pain. Unbearable, searing pain.

She'd fisted the sheets of paper into a knot and cast them in her wastepaper bin. They'd sat there all day, a constant reminder of a man so hell-bent on revenge that he was incapable of listening to reason. The hands on her office clock had edged their way to 6:00 p.m. when she finally gave in. If she could give the Palmers one more strength, one more piece of armour in this battle between Josh and them, she'd darn well do it.

She smoothed out the sheets and took them straight through to Irene, who was still at her desk.

"I believe you might find these of some use."

"What are they?" Irene took the creased papers and set them in front of her, adjusting her reading glasses on the tip of her nose. She scanned them for a few minutes then looked up over the lenses. "Callie, you realise what these are, don't you?"

"Yes, I do. They were the last thing I worked on before…" she faltered.

She couldn't say the words without her throat closing up as if it had suddenly swollen on the lies she'd been forced to live in this desperate tussle between two families.

Irene removed her glasses and pinned Callie under her impenetrable grey stare. "I know this whole situation with Tremont asked a great deal more of you than we anticipated. You can't let it get to you, you know. If you're going to succeed in this world, you have to do what's right—and in this case you definitely did what is right."

Callie bit her lip. What was right for the Palmers, perhaps—but deep down she knew she hadn't succeeded. She hadn't managed to burn all the evidence Josh had against his father. He could still use it to publicly humiliate Bruce and ruin his appointment to Guildara before it happened, even if Palmers was now going to be in a stronger financial position with the Flinders contract secure, and now this one within its grasp.

Drawing on the example of the woman in front of her, Callie reassumed the mantle of icy suspension that had seen her survive the night.

"Thank you, Irene. Now, if that's all today, I think I'll head home."

Irene nodded her dismissal. On her drive home, Callie honed that icy calm into steel-plated armour. With any luck it would see her through the rest of her life because she knew to the soles of her feet that she would never allow herself to be so vulnerable ever again. It simply hurt too much. It was better to stay on the path she'd chosen. To be the best at her job she could be. To take comfort in casual friendships and leave life at that.

Maybe she'd get a cat, she thought. Something that could subsist beside her without expecting more than she was prepared to give, and without giving more than she could accept. But even as she dwelled on that thought, she knew she wouldn't. There was only one thing missing in her life—Josh—and without him she couldn't bear to accept any other substitute.

It was two weeks until Christmas and the joyful hymns and carols pumping through the building's elevators' sound system were already driving Callie nuts. She ascended to the executive floor and stepped out with relief, the assault in her eardrums and her psyche over. It was hard enough watching the world go by in a fever of excitement over a festival she normally avoided without it impinging on her workspace as well.

As soon as Callie reached her office, though, she knew something was terribly wrong. Adam Palmer waited for her by her desk. Callie had barely seen him since his marriage, but those times she had he'd been relaxed and happy in a way she'd never seen before. Now, though, tension vibrated through every line in his body, and her smile of welcome quickly faded from her face.

"Callie, come with me to the boardroom."

There was a coolness to his voice that made her stomach clench in fright. That and the realisation his words had not been couched as a request, but as a command.

"Adam, what's wrong?"

"We'll discuss it there," was all he'd say and Callie was left to follow his rigid back along the carpeted hallway.

From every empty office they passed she heard phones shrilling unanswered. Where was everyone? The board-room door, normally open, was firmly closed and a buzz of angry voices echoed through the wooden barrier.

Silence ensued as Adam pushed open the door.

"She's here."

Two words, yet they made her suddenly feel as if she were walking a plank over shark-infested waters.

"Sit down, please, Callie," he directed.

Callie did as she was told, her eyes skimming over the assembly of senior executives ranging opposite her. At either end of the table sat Irene and Bruce Palmer. Twelve sets of accusing eyes bored into her, making her fidget on her chair.

Adam took charge of the proceedings immediately.

"Is it true that during the time you were with Josh Tremont you entered into a personal relationship with him?"

Callie's eyes flew to Irene. What the heck? Irene had told her to do whatever it took, and she had—at great personal cost. Was she now to be denounced for it?

"I did, but I—"

"And is it true that you passed on information to Palmer Enterprises that enabled us to win the Flinders contract over Tremont Corporation." Adam's tone was relentless.

"I did what I was sent in there to do."

"The information you gave to my mother two weeks ago, who gave it to you?"

"Josh did, but—"

"Did he put you up to this? Did you do it deliberately?" one of the other executives interrupted before she could finish.

"Do you have any idea what this has cost us?" another shouted from across the polished expanse of mahogany.

"I don't know what you're talking about. What the heck is going on?"

Callie turned to Bruce and his grey features and aged expression shocked her to her core.

"The information you gave to Irene was a setup, Callie. We're going to lose millions—maybe everything." Bruce's voice cracked on the last couple of words.

Callie swallowed against the sudden dryness in her throat. The information was false? They were losing millions? Palmers wasn't in a position to lose millions, not after losing so much business to Tremont Corporation already. She'd believed that the Flinders deal, together with the latest information she had, would give them the boost they'd needed. To get them back on par with Tremont Corporation. But instead she'd dragged them into a quagmire.

Realisation dawned with damning finality. Josh had set her up. He'd set her up to take the Palmers down. To make them take the fall he'd been engineering all along.

Black spots swam before her eyes and her chest constricted on a breath that simply could not be taken. Her eyes flew to Irene.

"But *you* know I wouldn't do anything to hurt you, to hurt Palmers. I was doing what you asked me to do. I uncovered the mole here, who was feeding information to Josh Tremont. I brought you the Flinders information."

"The results, unfortunately, speak for themselves," Adam said. "I'm sorry, Callie, but you know the process. Pending a full investigation, you're being stood down from your job."

Nothing in his voice betrayed the camaraderie they used to share. No hint of what had been a strong friendship, before she'd started to even work for his mother, remained.

Callie's eyes flew back and forth across the table, settling on Irene. Silently, she beseeched the older woman to support her, to tell them they were wrong. To make it clear that she would never deliberately do anything to hurt the family.

"Irene?" she implored.

Irene wouldn't meet Callie's eyes and Callie knew in that instant she'd not only been set up by Josh, she'd

been the fall guy for Irene Palmer at the same time.
What a fool she'd been to think she mattered to anyone.
She was little more than collateral damage in a power
play she'd never stood a chance of understanding. All
these years she'd believed she was worth something to
Irene, worth something to Palmers, yet all along she'd
been expendable. Groomed to do a job and discarded
when she was no longer useful.

Her devastation was complete. And to think that
she'd wanted to protect Irene from the proof of her
husband's infidelity. How naive could she have been?
If the cool derision on Irene's face right now was any
indicator, she probably had known about Bruce's affair
all along.

Adam motioned to someone outside the boardroom.
The blur of blue that denoted one of the security team
materialised beside her.

"Callie, I'm sorry. But we have to do it this way."
Adam followed her and the security guard out of the
boardroom, his voice tinged with genuine regret. "If
there was anything else I could do—"

"You could believe me, Adam. You could believe
that I am the innocent party here," she pleaded.

"I do believe you, Callie. And, trust me, I'll find a
way to get to the bottom of this. At the very least I'll
make sure you get a strong reference."

Callie looked back into the boardroom—at the ac-
cusation painted on many of the faces there, at the
distance she now knew lay between herself and the
woman she'd considered a mentor and friend.

"Good luck with that," she said bitterly.

In a state of numbed resignation, Callie allowed herself to be escorted from the building and down to the parking garage to her car, and as she drove out into the bustle of Auckland, she knew her life would never be the same again.

A burst of rage bloomed inside. Rage at Irene for letting her take the fall for what she'd been asked—no, had been *expected*—to do. Irene had manipulated her just as effectively as Josh Tremont had. She'd trusted both of them, and in doing so it had allowed each to play her like a puppet in a sideshow.

She hadn't even been given an opportunity to present her side of the story. The unfairness of it all settled like a ball of lead in her stomach. She'd sacrificed her relationship with Josh to protect them, to protect Irene and Bruce, and ultimately Adam and everyone who worked at Palmers. Yet she'd failed spectacularly.

She tried to rationalise the fact that if Palmers hadn't been so hungry and hell-bent on getting ahead of Tremont Corporation, in a competition that had become decidedly unhealthy, they'd have taken the time to thoroughly and carefully analyse Josh's notes and see for themselves the pitfall they'd rushed headlong into. Their greed had overrun their good sense, but, ultimately, she was responsible. She was the one who'd given them the information, no matter how fallacious it had turned out to be. Information that had been given to her in confidentiality. Whatever Josh's intentions had been when he'd made those notes, she and only she had been the one to abuse them. She had made the conscious decision to pass the information across to Palmers.

It was a frightening thought. She'd become so determined to be accepted, on being part of a whole, she'd compromised her own integrity. First with Josh and then with Irene. Yes, they'd used her, but she'd let them. And that was the most galling of all.

It was time to stand on her own two feet. To stand up for what she believed in and what was right. No more being a pawn in the hands of others.

Somehow, some way, she was going to undo the harm she'd done. And she would start with Josh Tremont.

Twelve

"I must see him."

He heard her voice as he crossed the lobby. Callie tapped her foot impatiently on the tiles where she stood at the visitor check-in area of the Tremont Tower.

"Ms Lee, Mr Tremont made it quite clear that you are not permitted on the premises." The security guard behind the desk held firm on his stance.

"C'mon, Ted, please. I need to talk to him. Get him on the phone for me."

"That won't be necessary."

She visibly flinched at the tone of his voice. Good, he thought. She had no right to be here and if his speech was enough to rattle her then she'd be gone all the sooner.

"Thank you, Ted. I'll take care of Ms Lee. It should only take a few minutes."

Josh wrapped his fingers around the top of Callie's bare arm, ignoring the warmth of her soft skin beneath his touch and the reminder of how soft her skin was all over her body. He staunchly reminded himself that this encounter was unfortunate, but unavoidably necessary. Clearly, she hadn't understood him when he'd sent her away.

He all but frog-marched her to the elevator bank and into a waiting car. He swiped his card in the reader and hit a button. As the doors closed them into the isolation of the car Josh faced her. He knew the expression on his face was anything but friendly.

"What are you doing here?" he demanded.

"Why aren't we going up to your floor?" Callie countered.

"You wanted to talk to me. You have my undivided attention for the next five minutes. Now, talk."

"You used me."

"As you did me. Call it even." He crossed his arms and assumed an expression of boredom. "Is that it?"

"No, that's not it."

Anger suited her—her brown eyes, usually doelike and sexy, hardened and shone like dark polished cherrywood. He tried to keep his observation on a dispassionate level, but the primal beat of his libido shouted him down. Even as distant as he attempted to remain, face-to-face she still affected him on a base level he couldn't control. And knowing that made him need to withdraw even more.

He raised one brow and waited for her to continue.

"You deliberately fed me information that would damage Bruce Palmer."

"You gave it to them."

"How could you do that?"

"Business." He sighed, "Look, this is a waste of time. You made it quite clear the other night where your loyalties lie and they're not with me. The fact you gave them the information you did is proof positive."

And that, he admitted, hurt more than he'd been prepared for. The past two weeks had been hell. He hadn't even begun to look for a new assistant. This close to Christmas who could be bothered anyway? No, he needed to be honest. He'd tried to tell himself he didn't trust anyone else to work alongside him, but it was much more than that.

He'd missed Callie with an aching need that he didn't want to begin to examine. The last time he'd felt so bereft, so lost, had been when his mother died. But Callie was nothing like his mother. It hadn't been difficult to remind himself of that.

"What happened with your employers is no more than what they deserved."

"Was everything a lie, Josh?"

He looked at her and bit back the retort that flew to his lips. She should know all about lies.

She closed the short distance between them and

laid a hand on his chest, her slender fingers curving over his heart.

"We had something there. Something special. I know I screwed up, but please. Won't you hear it from my side—my reasons why?"

"You and I have nothing further to discuss. You took your job with me under false pretences. You abused a position of trust to feed information back to people you knew were my enemy both personally and profession-ally. Why the hell should I believe that whatever else we shared was any different?

"To be honest, you went above and beyond the call of duty by sleeping with me. I don't think even Irene Palmer could have expected that of you."

He didn't miss the look on Callie's face and felt ice form deep inside his chest at the truth he saw reflected there. He took her hand and removed it from him.

"So, she *did* expect that of you. And like a well-trained puppet you did exactly as she said. Well, I hope they're looking after you, Callie. You're quite the employee of the month."

"I told you before. I couldn't have done that if I hadn't been falling in love with you. I'm not like that."

"I believe you mentioned food and shelter once before. However you dress it up, this was no different."

"Josh," her voice broke, "I love you."

"Then I'm sorry for you, because I could never love anyone I didn't trust and I do not trust you."

Even as he spoke he felt a shaft of pain as a shadow of longing died deep inside. He released the lock on the elevator and the doors opened. As she walked away, he gritted his teeth and forced himself to hit the button that would close the doors and shoot him skyward to his office, to where she still lingered even though he'd ordered her things removed and her desk cleared.

It was over—the damage had been done. Which left one last task on his list.

Josh tossed the morning newspaper onto his breakfast table in disgust. Couldn't they find anything better to report in the lead-up to Christmas? Did speculation about the consul appointment to Guildara really warrant such intense coverage?

Really, he didn't know why he was so at odds. The media coverage was heightening interest. Interest that would fly off the Richter scale when he exposed the prime candidate for the kind of man he really was.

He stalked through to the living room and snatched his mother's chest off the bookcase. He flipped it open; he hadn't bothered to lock it again. What was the point? It was as if by locking it he could keep what had happened shut away inside, allowing it to fester and grow.

But the time had come to let it go. To use what was there and finally achieve some form of recompense for his mother's hardship, and her early death. Today was the day he'd planned to release the letters to the media. He'd have bet his entire fortune on the fact they'd be falling over one another to decry the man they feted now.

He should just send the letters to the national newspaper and be done with it. Then he could just sit back and anticipate Bruce Palmer's very public downfall with a deep satisfaction. Yet somehow, the satisfaction in what he knew would be the ultimate outcome was lacking. Against his will, Callie's words to him echoed in his mind.

Promise me you'll read the letters again. Really read them this time.

Unable to ignore the compulsion any longer, he carefully lifted the first of the less seriously damaged envelopes he'd retrieved and, after setting the box back on the shelf, gingerly slid the letter out from inside.

He dropped down into an easy chair and unfolded the charred sheet of paper, his fingers blackening as they held its damaged edges. His eyes roamed over the words. Words of love from a married man to his mother. Words that promised the earth, together with an undying love.

Josh finished the letter and reached for the next.

Ten minutes later his eyes burned as he read the second to last letter in the box. He was suffering eyestrain, that's all it was, he told himself. But deep down he knew he couldn't lie to himself anymore. With the maturity of his years and without the rawness of teen grief, he'd read the letters in a new light.

With each one his anger had lessened a degree. His bitterness paled. There were nuances in the letters he'd totally missed the first time he'd read them. Nuances that spoke volumes as to how miserable and unhappy Bruce had been in his marriage to Irene.

They weren't the words of a man to a woman he saw as a casual fling. Every letter he'd addressed "To my dearest, Suzanne" and he'd signed off "Yours forever, Bruce." While the rest of her life had undoubtedly been hard, his mother had genuinely known love. For that alone, Josh could find a glimmer of gratefulness.

Had Bruce Palmer really planned to leave his wife, as he'd promised? To make a new life with Josh's mother? It had certainly appeared to be so. But what had happened to kill that? To have him send her away so callously?

Josh set down the letter he'd been reading and reached inside the box for the final envelope. He extracted the typewritten note on an early version of Palmer Enterprises letterhead and the company cheque that his mother had never deposited.

How had Bruce gone from a man devotedly in love to the cold, calculating creature who had sent this letter and cheque? Telling Suzanne to leave and to never show her face again. It just didn't make sense, but it had made enough sense to his mother that she'd packed her bags and checked out of the boardinghouse where she'd stayed in Auckland, and seen her catch the first bus south.

He stared blankly at the now rusty staple that still attached the cheque to the letter and idly flipped the paper to look again at the sum of money Bruce Palmer had thought worth getting rid of his mistress forever. A paltry sum in today's terms, but it would have made a difference for his mother back then.

It didn't matter anymore. Nothing mattered anymore. Suzanne was dead and no amount of revenge would bring her back.

Josh went to scoop the letters up and put them back in the box, but something stilled his hand. A niggle in the back of his mind that wouldn't let go.

He picked up the letter with the cheque attached and studied it anew.

"Well, I'll be damned," he said to the empty room.

He hadn't expected Irene Palmer to agree to see him so easily, but it seemed that whoever was acting as her assistant these days had no idea he was persona non grata in the exalted Palmer Enterprises building. The looks he'd received on his way up to Irene's office would have made him laugh out loud had he not been so hell-bent on reaching his destination.

But those looks were nothing compared to the expression on her face when he was shown through to her office.

"Your ten o'clock is here, Mrs Palmer." The fresh-faced secretary who'd made his appointment showed him directly into her domain.

"My ten…" Irene rose from her chair. "You! Call security, Anna. This man should not be here."

"I think you'll find you do want to see me, Irene."

Josh slid the typewritten letter and cheque from his pocket and opened it out on the desk in front of her. He could almost have felt sorry for her as the colour drained from her face and she slumped back into her chair.

"Mrs Palmer? Do you still want me to call security?"

The younger woman sounded scared. Josh was prepared to lay money on the fact that probably no one had ever seen Irene Palmer at a disadvantage before.

"No, not any more," Irene rasped through lips that had turned slightly blue around the edges. "Please close the door on your way out."

As soon as the door shut behind her assistant, Irene appeared to summon courage from somewhere. Josh had to admit to a grudging admiration. Not many people could recover from a shock like the one she'd just received with such aplomb. Even seated she managed to convey that she was looking down her nose at him. That he was nothing more than a piece of gum stuck to the bottom of her heel.

"So *you're* her son," she finally said, almost to herself. "Now it all makes sense."

Without waiting for her invitation, which he doubted would be forthcoming anyway, he settled his frame in one of the button-back leather chairs that faced her desk. "Just what did you say to my mother to make her leave?"

"What makes you think I said anything?"

"Don't patronise me, Irene. We both know it wasn't Bruce who sent her away. That's your signature on that cheque."

Irene seemed to shrivel a little under his stare.

"It was pathetically easy, you know. Mind you, so was she."

Josh clenched his jaw against the fury her deliberate insult roused inside him. He took strength in the secure knowledge that her words were a lie. His mother had never been easy. She'd been a devoted mother and she'd been a lady. And if she'd ever craved male companionship after her affair with Bruce, she quelled that craving, putting Josh's needs ahead of her own every day of his life.

When he didn't visibly react to her comment, Irene continued.

"Bruce and I had difficulty starting a family. After ten years, we'd all but given up hope—the failure created a distance between us. In many ways it was a relief when he turned to her for comfort, and I was always grateful for his discretion. He knew if a scent of his relationship with her leaked out how destructive it would have been to me. No one else ever knew.

"When I unexpectedly became pregnant I knew I had to fight to keep him and I was determined to win. I hadn't strived to build all of this," she gestured across her office with her hand, "with my husband to see it all crumble for the sake of Bruce's little fling with his secretary.

"I knew my pregnancy gave me the ammunition to get Bruce to give her up, until I noticed something else. Your mother made all her own clothes and it didn't take an expert eye to see that she'd begun to slowly let the seams out on her dresses, or to recognise the fragility in her face. I stared at the same weakness in myself every morning."

"So you confronted her."

"Yes, I confronted her. You think I was going to let her

destroy what Bruce and I had created for our own children? Bruce is the type of man who would have stood by her; he would have given her child—*you*—everything our own boys deserved. There was no way I would allow my children's birthright to be diluted by her bastard."

Irene shoved her chair back from her desk and began to pace.

"I knew she couldn't have told him about her pregnancy yet, or Bruce would have made a move by then to leave me, and I wasn't about to be upstaged. So I went to see her in that revolting boardinghouse where she lived and told her it was over. That Bruce had confessed his affair to me but that he no longer loved her."

Irene laughed then, a brittle sound that grated on Josh's ears.

"I told her Bruce wanted her to leave Auckland. She refused, telling me she knew Bruce loved her. Loved *her!* But I convinced her in the end. I gave her the letter and the cheque and told her to use it to get rid of the baby she was carrying. That night I went home and I told Bruce I was pregnant. He was overjoyed, and the rest, as they say, is history. Oh, he tried to find her, to let her down gently, I suppose, but she was already gone. Well and truly gone, and good riddance."

No wonder his mother had never cashed that cheque. It had been blood money. Money for the sole purpose of taking a life that had been conceived in love. That Bruce had loved Suzanne he had absolutely no doubt. He'd read the letters. He'd seen the fear in Irene's eyes. It was a fear that still ruled her.

Josh's hands curled into knotted fists as he sat and listened to Irene's invective. The woman was poison. She'd played with lives, moving them around as if they were no more than pieces on a chessboard.

"You sent that letter to me when my mother died, when I tried to let Bruce know."

"Of course I did. I'd protected my family for more than eighteen years from that woman. Do you really think I was going to be less vigilant after all that time?"

"He had a right to know she'd gone. He had a right to know *me*."

"My husband will never acknowledge you as his son," she stated, her voice as frigid as the Great Southern Ocean.

"That doesn't matter to me anymore, Irene, because, you see, even though you thought you'd done everything right to protect your precious family, you—and only you—have sown the seeds of the destruction of what you tried hardest to save."

"How dare you! You're the one. You're the mastermind behind it all. You even used that poor girl to further your maniacal scheme."

"If, by *poor girl,* you're talking about Callie, then maybe you should ask yourself why you groomed her for so many years and then let her take the blame when everything turned upside down. What kind of person scouts for the vulnerable the way you did with her, and then lets her believe she belongs—that she has a place in your world? Then, when it no longer suits you, you cast her adrift as if she has no value to you anymore. Is that how you measure everyone in your life? By what they can do for you?"

Josh closed his eyes a moment to compose himself. To draw on every last ounce of control he had left. "I feel sorry for you, Irene, because when all is said and done you had to cheat and lie to get what you have today—your husband, your business, your entire world. All of it based on lies. You say you've done it to protect your family, but you only did what you did out of fear. Fear of rejection, fear of failure. And when the truth comes out, who will stand in your corner then?"

Twin spots of colour stood stark on Irene's cheeks, but he could see the fear that now reflected in her eyes. Could see that she feared *him* and the threat he was to the very fabric of her world.

"You're threatening me with the media? I'll have an injunction slapped on you so fast you won't know what gagged you. You will not spoil my plan. Palmer Enterprises will recover from your attempt to destabilise us, and when Bruce and I move to Guildara, he'll be the jewel in their diplomatic crown because I protected him from *you*."

"No. I'm not going to the media. Not any more. Nor am I going to systematically take Palmer Enterprises apart piece by piece. You're simply not worth the effort. Besides, I think my father and my half brother deserve better than that. But what you decide to do next will be the key to what makes or breaks Palmers and your dreams for the future. And if your entire world falls apart, you will know that you were the only one who could have done anything about it. See how you like playing God with that truth."

How he made it out the office and down in the elevator to the entrance to the building he didn't know, but the moment he stepped free of the Palmer Enterprises building he knew a freedom he had never experienced before.

Freedom tinged with grief for the ill-fated love affair his parents had shared. For so many years he'd believed his father had been a man to be vilified. Some all-powerful being that had held Josh's fate, and the eventual fate of his mother, in his hands. Yet all along he'd been a victim of his world. A man who'd been too late—and yes, maybe even too weak—to act when love had been his for the taking.

Yet, despite that, Bruce had given Suzanne happiness, even if only for a short time. And it said a lot that his mother had never once run his father down. Never once apportioned blame. To her dying day, he knew she must have loved him and that kind of love was a gift, no matter how long you shared it.

An ache started deep in Josh's chest. He'd had the chance to know that kind of love. Callie had offered it to him, and he'd cast it back in her face like a handful of bad stock options.

Josh strode to the nearby taxi stand. He couldn't afford the time to retrieve his car from the parking lot nearby. Too many mistakes had been made already in the name of greed. He wasn't about to make another.

Thirteen

Callie ignored the demand of her doorbell. She wasn't in the mood for theological discussion or the latest multibuy bargain card. Not today—not ever.

Since she'd been summarily suspended from Palmer Enterprises, she'd lived in a kind of limbo—lacking even the energy to bother to dress each day. And underlying her miserable existence lay a sense of loss and pain and "what ifs," making sleep patchy at best during the darkest hours of the night.

The door chimed again, and still she ignored it.

"Come on, Callie. I know you're in there."

Josh? What did he want? Hadn't he made his position clear enough already? Whatever it was, she wasn't up for any more emotional abuse. She'd ignore him. Eventually, he'd go away.

This time when the doorbell rang it was continuous. Her eardrums vibrating with the noise, she pounded down her stairs and flung her front door open.

"What? Ready to go another round with me? Well, I'm all out of fight so get out of my face."

"Last time we talked you wanted to tell me your side of things. I wasn't ready to listen to you then. I am now."

"Oh, so everything is all on your timetable. I'm so sorry," she said, her voice dripping with a sarcasm that did little to mask the pain throbbing through her at the sight of him. "I don't have time in my busy schedule of unemployment."

"Callie, please."

Josh stepped across the threshold, forcing her to back up to avoid the breadth and strength of him. She should feel threatened by his mass, but instead all her traitorous body wanted to do was plaster itself against him. Feel his heat and hardness and envelop herself in it until she felt no pain, only sensation.

The snick of the front door closing made her take another step back.

"Tell me," he prompted.

There was a note of sincerity in his voice that gave her pause. He wasn't the kind of man to ask if he didn't mean it and he also wasn't the type to leave until he got the answers he sought. With a shrug of resignation, she led him through to her kitchen, where she grabbed her kettle from its stand and shoved it under the tap.

"Coffee?"

"If you're having some."

She grunted and dealt with the necessities of getting coffee ready. Instant, not percolated. She wasn't going to any bother for a man who'd chewed her up and spit her out twice in the past month. And she'd let him. She'd set herself up that second time by going to him. By hoping she could appeal to his better nature. The nature she knew dwelled inside the focussed businessman who dominated his market like some feudal lord.

Eventually, she pushed a mug across the kitchen table toward him, paying no regard to the brown liquid sloshing over the sides.

If she'd had any pride left it might have bothered her that her hair was a tangle of unbrushed chaos and that her sleep shorts and tank top had seen better days. Her attire was a far cry from the nightgown she'd worn the last time they'd made love. A tight knot wadded up deep inside her. She didn't want to think about that night, about what they'd shared. About how they'd given to one another, and taken—both overcome by an insatiable hunger.

She'd had plenty of time to think about that and she was done thinking. She knew she'd acted foolishly, impulsively. But she'd loved him with her heart, her mind and her body—and he'd taken that love and used it against her.

"Where do you want to begin?" he asked, taking a sip of the coffee and ignoring the drips from the base of the mug that splattered onto his Armani suit.

"Why now, Josh? You weren't interested before," she hedged. She wasn't in a hurry to rip the scab off the emotional wounds that had finally healed and been tucked away.

"Because I was wrong. You were right. I realise that now. I was driven by anger and frustration over something I knew next to nothing about. Something I didn't even have the maturity to understand. It did twist me up inside and make me bitter and both unwilling and unable to see anything from anyone's point of view but mine."

He put his mug down on the table and sighed.

"I did what you suggested. I read the letters again. Really read them this time. How I didn't see what my mother meant to him the first time around I'll never understand."

"You were too lost in your own grief. You can't be too hard on yourself."

"Whether that's true or not I should never have let it guide my entire life. It turned me into someone I don't even like anymore."

"I still love you." The words slipped from her mouth before she even realised she'd said them aloud.

"I don't deserve your love, Callie. You deserve better than me, more than what I can give you."

"Josh, if you could have given me your love in return that would have been enough. I know what it's like not to have love. My parents never wanted children. When I came along, it certainly wasn't the unexpected bonus their friends told them it was. They gave me the bare necessities of life, barely tolerated me when I was around. Sure, they made certain I was fed and dressed and sent to school. But they never wanted me.

"They loved each other and yet they hated each other, too. Their relationship was symbiotic and destructive at the same time. They both drank, excessively, and they did recreational drugs, too. My mother was the worst. She'd lash out when she was angry and she was angry a lot of the time. When she didn't get the response, or the respect, from me she believed she was due, she'd change from shouting and verbal abuse to physical violence. My father did nothing to stop her.

"The day I turned fourteen, she beat me worse than she'd ever done before. They had to call an ambulance, but neither of them came to the hospital with me. When the doctors saw my injuries they called the police, but by the time they arrived at our house my parents had left. No one knew where they had gone. I'm assuming they fled the country. We didn't have the border control then that we do now."

Callie fell silent, remembering the visit from the social worker telling her that she'd now be a ward of the state and remembering her silent vow not to be under anyone's control ever again.

"Anyway, as soon as I was well enough I checked myself out of hospital and hit the streets. It wasn't hard to disappear in the underground community, to learn when to duck and hide and when it was safe."

"Social services never looked for you?"

"They probably did, but it didn't take long before I

became adept at my new lifestyle and it was easier than what had been before. I survived for two years before things got seriously dangerous for me. That was when Irene's people found me."

"More dangerous than living on the street? Callie, you were what by then? Sixteen?"

She looked at Josh across the table. For all the hardship in his upbringing he really had no idea how gruelling life could really be. At least he'd had his mother.

"My last winter on the street was more difficult than the previous two. Wetter, colder—just altogether more miserable. There was a guy I was soft on. He didn't live on the streets but he spent a lot of time there. That should have been a warning to me, but it wasn't. Anyway, he'd always been out of my league but this one night he actively sought me out and he offered to take me back to his place for the night. I knew exactly what that meant—and I hate to admit it now—but I was so cold, so tired and so darn hungry I would have done just about anything for warmth and clean sheets that night. So I went with him."

Her voice faded away on the memory, on the bitter cold and desolation. She became aware of heat encasing her hands. Of Josh's silent encouragement and support chasing away the fear and the bad memories.

"I found out later that he wasn't as young as he looked. But he used his youthful appearance to scout for young girls and had quite a business running with them once he got them totally dependent on him and the drugs he pushed. I was one of the lucky ones. The police raided the next morning and I was sent to one of Irene's facilities."

She transferred her grip from her mug to Josh's hands, entwining her fingers through his as if by doing so she could impart the truth of what she was telling him.

"She saved me, Josh. She saved me and made me whole again. She made me see that I could be anything I wanted to be, do anything I wanted to do if I just wanted it enough. I owed her everything."

"And she took it. She used you and abandoned you when you needed her most."

"I'm nothing if not consistent," Callie said bitterly. "Never let it be said that I inspire loyalty in the people in my life."

"You do in me."

"No, I don't. I failed you, too."

"None of us are perfect, but you could see before I did that I was wrong and that what I was doing was wrong. You have so much courage, Callie, you almost frighten me. You stood up to me, not just once, but twice. You stood up for what you believed in—me. And that's a gift I want to keep forever—you, your love. Can you ever forgive me?"

"Have you really let it go? The anger? Your need for revenge?"

"I'll be honest. I found out some truths today that re-directed my anger. Irene separated my mother and Bruce—she was the one who sent Mum away and gave her money, she was the one who intercepted my letter when I wrote to say Mum had died. Irene had just discovered she was pregnant and she didn't want her child or children to be usurped. She persuaded my mother that Bruce didn't love her anymore and she sent her away. Irene was behind everything—she's one evil manipulative woman. I'm not going to let her infect my life with her vitriol any longer. And she's not going to contaminate yours, either."

"And Bruce? What about the letters."

"I thought I'd destroy them. Leave them in the past where they belong. Or maybe we should return them to him. They're his property in the end, aren't they?"

Callie could barely believe her ears. He really had let all that anger go? It had been his direction for so long; it had been a part of what sculpted him into the man he was. Letting go would leave a void in his life, a loss of purpose.

"I think whatever you decide will be fine," she answered carefully.

"So do I have your forgiveness?"

"Of course you do. But can you forgive me? I lied to you; I deliberately tried to undermine your plans."

"I love you, Callie, even if I hadn't already been in the wrong I could forgive you for anything as long as I know I had your love in return."

Tears sprang to her eyes and she dashed them away as happiness swelled to an almost unbearable peak within her.

"You do, oh, yes, you do. I love you, Josh. I always will."

"Then come home with me. Stay with me, be my

wife. Let's create the family we both always wanted. The family we both deserve."

"I'll do it on one condition," she said, smiling through tears of joy.

"Name it. It's yours."

"Will you call me Callie Rose?"

"Always."

He stood and pulled her from her chair, into his arms where she finally belonged, and he took her love from her lips and into his body, holding it deep inside. She returned his kiss, and his faith in a happier future, with everything she had inside, and when she took him upstairs to her bedroom it was to show him with her body, her love, exactly what he meant to her.

Sunlight slanted through the cedar blinds in her bedroom window, encasing them both in a brilliant golden glow, a portent of hope in two lives that had known so much despair. She slid his clothes from his body, skimming her fingers over the width of his shoulders, the broad strength of his chest, tracing each line of muscle, sensing through her fingertips each shiver of his reaction.

When they were both naked, she led him to her bed and continued her exploration of his body, loving how his skin danced beneath her touch. Loving him. And when she knelt over him, and took him into her body, she felt a closeness with Josh that had been missing before. Finally, there were no secrets between them. Finally they could give and take without any shadows of the past lingering between them.

As she rose and fell against him, sensation swelled

upon pleasure, pleasure upon sensation, until they both tumbled over the edge of reality and onto a plane of pure joy, pure enlightenment. Pure love.

Later, as their bodies cooled and their breathing returned to normal, Callie relished the sound of Josh's heartbeat beneath her cheek—the heart that beat for her. For all they'd been through, for all they'd done, they'd made it through together and would each be stronger for that now.

Josh's fingers drew lazy circles against her back. She could stay in this half world forever, she thought with a smile. But then again, they'd have plenty of these times together. They had a lifetime to look forward to.

"You know," she said quietly, "I feel sorry for her."

"Irene?" Josh's voice was a deep rumble in her ear. "She doesn't need your pity."

"Yes, I think she does. She did help me, Josh. I know she cast me to the wolves when everything began to crumble, but deep down I really feel sorry for her. She only fought for what she believed in—her family, their security, their future. Really, what she did was not a lot different from what you did to them. It's like everything came full circle."

Josh lay silent beneath her for several minutes before speaking.

"I hate to admit it, but you're right. The difference being, though, that I withdrew before it was too late."

"So you're definitely not going public with Bruce being your father?"

"No. I'm not even going to approach him about it.

I'm satisfied knowing he truly loved my mother. At least she had that, no matter how long it lasted."

Callie lifted her head and met Josh's gaze, saw the unexpected sheen of tears in his eyes.

"I love you, Josh Tremont. I don't deserve you, but I love you and I promise you I will love you until the day I die."

"That's all I ever wanted," he said, as he rolled her under him and lowered his face to her. "And you need never doubt I will spend every day of the future loving you exactly the same way."

By the time they'd spent their afternoon making love, packing enough of Callie's things to fit in her car, and making love again, it was early evening before they made it to Josh's place. As they reached the entrance to his drive, Callie noticed that the gates were open.

"Did you leave them open today?" she asked.

"I was in a hurry this morning."

"There's a car outside your house."

They cruised down the driveway, toward the dark Mercedes parked in the large turning bay. A Mercedes that Callie realised was very familiar. Her breath caught in her throat and a bundle of nerves clenched into a knot at the pit of her stomach. Josh slowed her car to a halt and got out.

The knot in Callie's stomach tightened even more when the driver's door on the Mercedes swung open and Bruce Palmer stepped out. If she'd thought he looked as if he'd aged the other day in the boardroom it was nothing compared to how he looked now.

His skin was grey and hung from his cheeks in folds, his eyes were red-rimmed, his posture stooped and his normally immaculate suit rumpled.

Through Josh's open door, she heard the older man's voice tremble as he spoke.

"Irene told me. Is it true? Are you my son?"

"Yes." Josh's voice choked on the word.

Grief and joy flew across Bruce Palmer's face and tears streaked down his cheeks. "My boy!"

The two men moved together as one, their arms outstretched one moment and clasped around one another the next as if nothing could ever tear them apart.

And as Callie watched Bruce hold his firstborn son for the very first time, she knew that finally everything would be all right. The great knot inside her unravelled and she got out of the car to follow them inside.

After making the men coffee, Callie left them alone together and took her things upstairs. She put everything away and then, loath to interrupt Josh and his father in their first chance to get to know each other, she moved outside, onto the main bedroom balcony. She looked down the hill and out to the water and wondered how they were doing. How they were coping with discovering each other as father and son.

She didn't hear Josh come up behind her. She simply felt his warmth and strength against her back, his arms sliding around her waist. She leaned back against his chest.

"He had to go. The Guildarian consulate function is tonight, but he wants to come over tomorrow—to spend part of Christmas Day with us. He said he's missed too many of them now to want to miss this one."

"So everything's okay?" she asked.

"Better than okay. I really didn't know how it would feel—to actually see him face-to-face. To have him acknowledge that he is my father. But it was incredible. He talked to me about Mum, about how he tried to find her after she'd gone, but she'd done too good a job of disappearing. He kept an eye on the electoral rolls for years, hoping she'd crop up and he'd then be able to make sure she was okay. In the end he concluded that she must have left the country." Josh took a deep breath and let it go in a rush of air. "I gave him the letters. I explained what you'd tried to do and we decided the best thing was to let them go. He finished what you started."

"I'm glad. They needed to be let go."

"Yeah. I know you can't hold on to the past forever. He's still very angry with Irene, but I know he will eventually forgive her. She finally told him the truth. Maybe they can start afresh when they move overseas. Who knows?"

"She had to protect what was hers. I know what she did came at a terrible cost to you and your mother, but she must have been desperately afraid of losing her husband. What's important is that she did the right thing in the end."

Josh pressed a kiss on the top of her head. "You're too soft, you know that?"

"Maybe I am, but it got me you, didn't it?"

"You're right. Maybe I do owe Irene something after

all. By the way, Bruce and I sketched up a plan to help Palmer Enterprises through the losses they've incurred with that erroneous deal I set up. With Bruce and Irene leaving for Guildara, I'll be working with Adam—my brother. My God, my brother! All these years I've envied him, even hated him for having everything I didn't, and now we'll be working together."

"Adam's a great guy—focussed. A lot like you really." Callie smiled. "You'll work well together—most of the time."

"Yeah, we're bound to bump heads every now and then, but we'll be working toward the same purpose, for a change." Josh nuzzled the side of Callie's neck. "It was good to talk to Bruce. We might never get to be as close as we could have been, but right now I feel as if the last pieces of my life have slotted into place, and it's all because of you."

"Me? How?"

"I came this close to ruining my own father and you stopped me. You made me question whether I was doing the right thing. I'll never be able to repay you for that, Callie."

"You don't need to repay me, just love me."

"I will always love you. Thank you. For everything."

As they turned together and walked back inside, Callie knew that this Christmas would be one they'd remember forever.

It was the start of the rest of their lives.

* * * * *

Bestselling author Lynne Graham is back with a fabulous new trilogy!

PREGNANT BRIDES

Three ordinary girls—naive, but also honest and plucky…

Three fabulously wealthy, impossibly handsome and very ruthless men…

When opposites attract and passion leads to pregnancy… it can only mean marriage!

Available next month from Harlequin Presents®: the first installment

DESERT PRINCE, BRIDE OF INNOCENCE

* * *

'THIS EVENING I'm flying to New York for two weeks,' Jasim imparted with a casualness that made her heart sink like a stone. 'That's why I had you brought here. I own this apartment and you'll be comfortable here while I'm abroad.'

'I can afford my own accommodation although I may not need it for long. I'll have another job by the time you get back—'

Jasim released a slightly harsh laugh. 'There's no need for you to look for another position. How would I ever see you? Don't you understand what I'm offering you?'

Elinor stood very still. 'No, I must be incredibly thick because I haven't quite worked out yet what you're offering me.…'

His charismatic smile slashed his lean dark visage. 'Naturally, I want to take care of you.…'

HPEX0110A

'No, thanks.' Elinor forced a smile and mentally willed him not to demean her with some sordid proposition. 'The only man who will ever take *care* of me with my agreement will be my husband. I'm willing to wait for you to come back but I'm not willing to be kept by you. I'm a very independent woman and what I give, I give freely.'

Jasim frowned. 'You make it all sound so serious.'

'What happened between us last night left pure chaos in its wake. Right now, I don't know whether I'm on my head or my heels. I'll stay for a while because I have nowhere else to go in the short term. So maybe it's good that you'll be away for a while.'

Jasim pulled out his wallet to extract a card. 'My private number,' he told her, presenting her with it as though it was a precious gift, which indeed it was. Many women would have done just about anything to gain access to that direct hotline to him, but his staff guarded his privacy with scrupulous care.

Before he could close the wallet, his blood ran cold in his veins. How could he have made such a serious oversight? What if he had got her pregnant? He knew that an unplanned pregnancy would engulf his life like an avalanche, crush his freedom and suffocate him. He barely stilled a shudder at the threat of such an outcome and thought how ironic it was that what his older brother had longed and prayed for to secure the line to the throne should strike Jasim as an absolute disaster....

* * *

What will proud Prince Jasim do if Elinor is expecting his royal baby? Perhaps an arranged marriage is the only solution! But will Elinor agree? Find out in DESERT PRINCE, BRIDE OF INNOCENCE by Lynne Graham [#2884], available from Harlequin Presents® in January 2010.

Copyright © 2010 by Lynne Graham

HPEX0110B

Have you discovered the Westmoreland family?

NEW YORK TIMES AND *USA TODAY*
BESTSELLING AUTHOR

BRENDA JACKSON

*Find out where it all started
with these fabulous 2-in-1 novels.*

On Sale December 29, 2009

Contains: *Delaney's Desert Sheikh*
and *Seduced by a Stranger* (brand-new)

On Sale January 26, 2010

Contains: *A Little Dare*
and *Thorn's Challenge*

www.kimanipress.com
www.myspace.com/kimanipress

KPBJW10SP

REQUEST YOUR FREE BOOKS!

2 FREE NOVELS PLUS 2 FREE GIFTS!

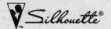 Silhouette® *Desire*®

Passionate, Powerful, Provocative!

YES! Please send me 2 FREE Silhouette Desire® novels and my 2 FREE gifts (gifts are worth about $10). After receiving them, if I don't wish to receive any more books, I can return the shipping statement marked "cancel". If I don't cancel, I will receive 6 brand-new novels every month and be billed just $4.05 per book in the U.S. or $4.74 per book in Canada. That's a savings of almost 15% off the cover price! It's quite a bargain! Shipping and handling is just 50¢ per book.* I understand that accepting the 2 free books and gifts places me under no obligation to buy anything. I can always return a shipment and cancel at any time. Even if I never buy another book, the two free books and gifts are mine to keep forever.   225 SDN EYMS 326 SDN EYM4

Name	(PLEASE PRINT)	
Address		Apt. #
City	State/Prov.	Zip/Postal Code

Signature (if under 18, a parent or guardian must sign)

Mail to the Silhouette Reader Service:
IN U.S.A.: P.O. Box 1867, Buffalo, NY 14240-1867
IN CANADA: P.O. Box 609, Fort Erie, Ontario L2A 5X3

Not valid to current subscribers of Silhouette Desire books.

**Want to try two free books from another line?
Call 1-800-873-8635 or visit www.morefreebooks.com.**

* Terms and prices subject to change without notice. Prices do not include applicable taxes. Sales tax applicable in N.Y. Canadian residents will be charged applicable provincial taxes and GST. Offer not valid in Quebec. This offer is limited to one order per household. All orders subject to approval. Credit or debit balances in a customer's account(s) may be offset by any other outstanding balance owed by or to the customer. Please allow 4 to 6 weeks for delivery. Offer available while quantities last.

Your Privacy: Silhouette Books is committed to protecting your privacy. Our Privacy Policy is available online at www.eHarlequin.com or upon request from the Reader Service. From time to time we make our lists of customers available to reputable third parties who may have a product or service of interest to you. If you would prefer we not share your name and address, please check here. ☐

SDES09R

Silhouette ® Desire

COMING NEXT MONTH
Available January 12, 2010

#1987 FROM PLAYBOY TO PAPA!—Leanne Banks
Man of the Month
Surprised to learn he has a son, he's even more surprised to learn
his ex-lover's sister is raising the boy. When he demands the child
live with him, he agrees to let her come too…as his wife.

#1988 BOSSMAN'S BABY SCANDAL—Catherine Mann
Kings of the Boardroom
What's an executive to do when his one-night stand is pregnant
and his new client hates scandal? Propose a temporary marriage,
of course. Yet their sizzling passion is anything but temporary.…

#1989 TEMPTING THE TEXAS TYCOON—Sara Orwig
He'll receive five million dollars if he marries within the year—
and a sexy business rival provides the perfect opportunity. But she
refuses to submit to his desires…especially when she discovers
his reasons.

**#1990 AFFAIR WITH THE REBEL HEIRESS—
Emily McKay**
Known for his conquests in the boardroom—and the bedroom—
the CEO isn't about to let his latest fling stand in his way. He'll
acquire her company, wild passion or not. Though he soon finds
out she has other plans in mind.…

**#1991 THE MAGNATE'S PREGNANCY PROPOSAL—
Sandra Hyatt**
She came to tell him the in vitro worked—she was carrying his
late brother's baby. When he drops the bomb that her baby is
actually *his,* he'll stop at nothing to stake his claim. Will she
let him claim *her?*

#1992 CLAIMING HIS BOUGHT BRIDE—Rachel Bailey
To meet the terms of his inheritance, he convinces her to marry
him. But can he seduce her into being his wife more than just
on paper?

SDCNMBPA1209